D0289365

SLEEPER AGENDA

Also by Tom Sniegoski

Sleeper Code

SLEEPER AGENDA

PART II
IN THE SLEEPER CONSPIRACY

TOM SNIEGOSKI

razOr
bill

Sleeper Agenda

RAZORBILL

Published by the Penguin Group
Penguin Young Readers Group
345 Hudson Street, New York, New York 10014, U.S.A.
Penguin Group (USA) Inc., 375 Hudson Street, New York,
New York 10014, U.S.A.
Penguin Group (Canada), 90 Eglinton Avenue, Suite 700, Toronto,
Ontario, Canada M4P 2Y3 (a division of Pearson Penguin Canada Inc.)
Penguin Books Ltd, 80 Strand, London WC2R 0RL, England
Penguin Ireland, 25 St Stephen's Green, Dublin 2, Ireland
(a division of Penguin Books Ltd)
Penguin Group (Australia), 250 Camberwell Road, Camberwell,
Victoria 3124, Australia (a division of Pearson Australia Group Pty Ltd)
Penguin Books India Pvt Ltd, 11 Community Centre, Panchsheel Park,
New Delhi - 110 017, India
Penguin Group (NZ), Cnr Airborne and Rosedale Roads, Albany,
Auckland 1310, New Zealand (a division of Pearson New Zealand Ltd)
Penguin Books (South Africa) (Pty) Ltd, 24 Sturdee Avenue,
Rosebank, Johannesburg 2196, South Africa

Penguin Books Ltd, Registered Offices: 80 Strand, London WC2R 0RL, England

10 9 8 7 6 5 4 3 2 1

Library of Congress Cataloging-in-Publication Data is available

Printed in the United States of America

For Richard J. Cunningham . . .

"Mr. Cunnigham, my mother, she married an Irishman."

"Oh really?"

"No, O'Reilly."

Once more for the road.

SLEEPER
AGENDA

PROLOGUE

Bodies—animal and human—were scattered about the dirt paths of the tiny Chukchi fishing village on the desolate shores of the Sea of Okhotsk.

Christian Tremain, director of field operations for the Pandora Group, felt an icy claw of fear slowly constrict around his heart as the Chinook helicopter banked to the left and began its descent to the inhospitable terrain.

"Whatever it was," Brandon Kavanagh said from beside him, "it worked fast."

Tremain didn't respond, slightly disturbed by the hint of excitement he heard in the voice of his acquisitions director. Instead, he focused his attention on the village below.

At precisely 0800 hours, an earthquake measuring 7.5 on the Richter scale had been detected in the northeastern region of the Siberian wilderness, namely, the Kamchatka Peninsula, a bleak, sparsely populated place. Ordinarily a quake like that would barely have generated an eyebrow raise from the Pandora Group, a covert agency whose sole purpose was to protect the United States from corrupt technologies developed throughout the world. But this village just so happened to be home to Vector 6, a biological warfare research station belonging to the former Soviet Union.

"We'll take a quick look at the village and then move on to Vector 6," Tremain said, slipping into his decontamination suit.

"Sounds like a plan." Kavanagh flipped the hood of his own protective garb over his head and face and secured it at his neck. He peered out through the clear plastic face mask, giving Tremain a thumbs-up.

The chopper landed with a bounce, and its back slowly dropped open. The security team, automatic weapons at the ready, were first to disembark, scanning the area for any threats—so far the Russians had been slow to respond, but who knew what kind of defenses they had set up around the village.

Tremain was next to descend, a cold blast of wind

from the Sea of Okhotsk chilling him through the light-weight fabric of the protective suit.

"Should've brought a sweater," Kavanagh joked as he followed with the two Pandora scientists, Drs. Martin Rigby and Stephanie Lane. The trio were laughing, joking about how Pandora was too cheap to buy decon suits with heating units.

Am I the only one who feels this? Tremain wondered. He looked through the faceplate of his suit at the frozen landscape and the tiny village ahead that seemed to have been dropped down in the midst of the cruel desolation of Siberia. *Overwhelming dread.*

The first bodies they found were those of a young man and his dog. It was apparent that death had come quickly, but judging by the expression frozen on the man's face, it had not been painless. The exposed flesh of his face and hands was covered with large, oozing sores.

"Looks a bit like smallpox," Kavanagh commented with a disturbing fascination. He knelt down and carefully unzipped the man's heavy coat, then unbuttoned the shirt to expose his chest. It too was covered with bloody pustules.

"It does and it doesn't," Lane answered. She set her metal briefcase down, flipped open the locks, and removed a culturette. "Death occurred in minutes; smallpox doesn't behave like that."

She used the cotton swab to collect some samples of drying fluid from one of the man's wounds.

"Could be a smallpox that's been genetically altered," Rigby suggested. The scientist picked up a scalpel, and Tremain looked away.

"It killed the dog as well," he said. Sores were visible around the animal's muzzle and on the bare flesh of its belly. "Looks like it kills indiscriminately—no species barrier." Tremain gently poked a dead bird close by with the toe of his suit.

"Interesting," he heard Kavanagh say, and glanced over to see that the acquisitions director was looking skyward, watching a flock of birds overhead. "Seems like our killer might have a time limit."

Rigby was placing something that he had collected from inside the man's nasal passages into his case. "That could very well have been built into the bug, like a fail-safe. If the virus only remains active for a specific amount of time, judging from when the earthquake hit, it must have spread within twelve hours. It allows for quicker deployment of troops within the kill zones—"

"Report, Commander," Tremain interrupted, addressing the head of the security team that had returned from the village. Even through their fogging face masks, he could see that they were upset.

"There are no survivors, sir," the combat-hardened soldier said, a slight tremble of emotion in his voice. "It's . . . it's pretty horrible."

"We did find something kind of unusual, sir," one of the female operatives stated. "Just behind that house, over there on the right." She pointed off into the village. "You might want to take a look."

The scientific team left the young man's body and walked into the village, careful not to tread on any fallen bodies, human or animal. There was an eerie silence that added to Tremain's sense of unease.

"It's over here, sir," the soldier directed, leading them past an old woman who had fallen ill in the doorway of her home. She clutched a wooden crucifix in her bloody hand.

Not even He *could help you against this,* Tremain thought, looking away to where the others had gathered, circling something lying on the ground. Carefully he made his way toward them.

"Don't think that those are native to this region," one of the soldiers was saying as Tremain squeezed between Kavanagh and Lane.

"Think we might have found our carrier," Rigby said.

A monkey lay dead on the ground, its sore-covered body twisted by rigor mortis, its mouth open in a silent scream of death. On one of its wrists was a plastic band with numbers and Russian letters written on it.

Kavanagh chuckled, his laugh sounding odd through the speakers in the hood of the decontamination suit. "Do you see the bracelet—can you read it?" he asked.

"My Russian's a little rusty," Tremain replied. "What's it say?"

"'Death's Kiss 75,'" Kavanagh read. "Our dead friend here was probably the test subject for the seventy-fifth version of this virus."

"Seventy-five versions of something that can do this." Tremain surveyed the death all around them.

"Practice makes perfect." Kavanagh turned away from the simian corpse. "I think it's time we get a look at Vector 6."

Vector 6 was a nondescript warehouse, less than a mile from the village across the desolate tundra. It could have been used by the villagers to store their fishing gear, but Pandora knew it had a far more sinister purpose.

The corrugated steel walls had crumbled in the earthquake, revealing a concrete bunker that seemed to grow up from the ground. It too was cracked, its foundation warped, and a security door hung open, swaying noisily in the biting wind.

Guns ready, the security team approached the bunker with caution. The commander stood in the entryway, shining his flashlight beam into the murky darkness.

"What do we have, Commander?" Tremain asked, moving to stand beside him.

A set of cracked stone stairs led down to a landing, where the bodies of two Soviet soldiers lay. As the team began to slowly descend, it became obvious that the soldiers had died from the same thing that had killed the villagers—the disease carried by the infected rhesus monkey.

Tremain found another heavy metal security door waiting for them at the landing. It had been twisted partially off its frame by the writhing of the earth. The opening wasn't large enough for an average-size human to pass through, but something small and dexterous could have easily escaped.

"Blow the door," Kavanagh suddenly instructed the security team. "We need to see what's inside."

Tremain looked at the man standing beside him. "Do you think that's wise, Brandon?"

Kavanagh's eyes seemed to twinkle as he watched the soldiers set up their explosives.

"We have to know what they've been up to here," he said, motioning the scientific team back up the stairs for cover.

"I say we detonate all of the explosives we've got—incinerate this entire warehouse and everything inside. Nothing good can ever come out of a place like this," Tremain said.

The first set of charges detonated, taking off the door, and they heard the sound of the metal falling heavily to the concrete landing.

Kavanagh looked at Tremain, a sly smile slowly forming as he turned and headed back down the stairs.

"All depends on how you define *good*," the director of acquisitions said, now standing before the entrance to Vector 6.

An ominous passage from his college days suddenly filled Tremain's thoughts as he watched the acquisitions director climb eagerly over the rubble through the blown security entrance. Tremain believed it was from Dante's *Inferno* and found the quote strangely appropriate as he watched Brandon Kavanagh pass through the doorway, swallowed by darkness.

Abandon hope, all ye who enter here.

CHAPTER 1

Killing was second nature. He was good at it, whether with a knife or a gun or even his hands; Tyler Garrett was a natural when it came to the art of murder.

And his skills were being put to the test this night as he approached the fenced encampment of the Brotherhood of the New Dawn—an anti-government militia group headquartered in Woolwine, Virginia. The group had been started back in the early nineties by a man named Elijah Cook, whose brother was slain during a raid by the government's Bureau of Alcohol, Tobacco, Firearms, and Explosives on the family farm several years earlier. Cook hated the U.S. government, and there was more than a passing suspicion that he was on the verge of perpetrating a terrorist act against the country.

Bright spotlights suddenly blinded Tyler, and he

raised a hand to protect his eyes. His assignment was simple: to get inside and do what he did best.

"Who's out there?" a voice yelled, and Tyler caught the sound of a shell being loaded into a shotgun.

He shivered and cowered in the glare of the spotlight. "I've come to see Father Cook," he cried, putting a tremble into his voice for effect. "Please, I have to speak to him—it's very important."

He squinted at the ground, trying to see beyond the intense light. He made out the shapes of two men approaching the gate, unlocking it, and then moving toward him. They were both armed—one with a shotgun, the other with a rifle. And by the way they carried themselves, the shifting of their body weight as they strode toward him, he guessed that they were carrying handguns as well.

"Please, it's important," Tyler begged as they came up to him.

One of the men stank of sweat and tobacco. He grabbed Tyler roughly, spun him around, and threw him to the dusty ground. It was hard not to react, but Tyler distracted himself with an amusing exercise where he tried to come up with as many creative ways to kill this guy and his partner as he could. As they wrapped the plastic restraints around his wrists, he was up to one hundred and thirty-five.

"This is private property, boy," the smelly one said. "And we don't take kindly to trespassers."

The man hauled Tyler to his feet by his bound wrists, nearly popping his arms from their sockets, but the teen endured—it was all part of the assignment.

The FBI suspected that Cook was involved in terrorist activities, but that was all they could do.

Suspect.

No matter how deeply they dug or how much surveillance they put him under, they could find nothing legally incriminating. Needless to say, the authorities were frustrated, their biggest fear being that Cook's plans were already in motion and they had no idea who or what his target or targets might be.

Which was how Tyler had become involved. His employer, Brandon Kavanagh, had once been part of the intelligence community, and although he no longer had any official standing in the government, he still maintained close ties. Kavanagh had heard about Cook's activities and had thought that this could be an interesting exercise for Tyler. Since they weren't bound by the constraints of the law, they could garner information where government agencies had failed. Tyler didn't mind—in fact, he thought it might be fun.

"My name is Brady Childs," Tyler lied. "My daddy is Ryan Childs—he's friends with Father Cook."

The man with the shotgun gave him a good shake while the other pointed his hunting rifle at him menacingly. Tyler instantly thought of twenty more ways to kill them.

"Father Cook don't like folks trespassing on his property in the middle of the—"

"The government took my daddy a few days ago— they're gonna ask him questions about Father Cook, about what he knows of the plans and all."

He watched as the expressions on the men's faces changed, nervous sidelong glances telling him that he'd struck a nerve.

The real Ryan Childs had been a close associate of Elijah Cook, although the two hadn't had any contact for a few years. Still, the idea that they might have shared important information wasn't all that far-fetched, which was why Tyler's bosses had arranged to have Childs, his wife, and his teenage son taken from their home in Alabama and hidden away until this assignment was completed.

Cook hadn't seen Childs's boy in over three years; the plan was for Tyler to pass himself off as Brady Childs long enough to get close to Cook. Then it wouldn't matter whether he uncovered the ruse or not.

"Hey, Mike, better give Father a call," the man

aiming the rifle said to the rank guard still holding Tyler's arms.

"Don't tell me what to do, Nate," Mike growled. "He said he didn't want to be disturbed unless it was an emergency."

Nate lowered his gun and scratched the top of his filthy John Deere baseball cap. "Well, I think this might be kinda important."

Mike seemed angry and took it out on Tyler, giving him a violent shake and poking his belly hard with the gun. "How'd you get here, Brady?" he asked. "I thought the Childses lived in Alabama."

"We do," Tyler responded, looking down at the gun held against his stomach. "Once my daddy got taken, I lit out and hit the road. I knew he'd want me to get to Father Cook and warn him."

The two sentries were silent, and Tyler could practically hear the gears turning in their stupid, backwoods heads as they tried to figure out what they should do. Tyler was getting antsy. He had a lot to do tonight and was anxious to get started.

Kavanagh had said that this would be his graduation test, a way to prove to the Janus Project that he was ready for the field. Sure, there had been other tests and he had passed with flying colors, but this would be his first assignment on American soil. That piece of information seemed to matter to Kavanagh, but as far as Tyler was concerned, killing was killing: he could do it on the moon and it would be the same.

"Goddammit," Mike barked. He removed a small walkie-talkie from his belt and turned away. "Papa Bear, this is Wolf Pack One. I know you didn't want to be disturbed and all, but we got ourselves a situation out here."

There was a crackling of dead air for a bit, and then a low, melodious-sounding voice answered. "What seems to be the problem, Wolf Pack One?"

"We got ourselves an intruder, sir." Mike looked over his shoulder, and Tyler tried to make himself appear as pathetic as possible.

"A kid; says he's Ryan Childs's boy. Says Childs's been taken by the law."

Again there was static-filled silence, then, "Bring him to me," and the signal was cut.

Nate smiled proudly as his partner returned. "See, I told you it was important. Maybe if you listened to me every once in a while—"

"Shut up," Mike snarled as he grabbed Tyler's elbow and steered him toward the gate.

Tyler had memorized the layout of the compound from notes and maps supplied by Kavanagh, but it wasn't the same as seeing it. It was as if Father Cook had set up his own little kingdom behind these fences. Men and women sat and chatted on the lighted front porches of prefabricated homes; the cry of a baby could be heard through one of the open windows. Other than the fence and the guards, there was nothing to indicate that these people were followers of a religious zealot plotting to destroy the government.

But who was he to talk? Many would probably argue that a teenage boy working as an operative for a highly secret, covert agency wasn't exactly the norm either.

Different strokes, he thought, allowing himself to be led to the larger of the buildings that he could see. This one wasn't a prefab; it was a nice, two-story home. Father Cook was lord and master, after all.

Tyler stumbled on the stairs, crying out as he banged his shins on the wooden steps.

"Get up, boy," Mike snapped, pulling him roughly to his feet.

He was continuing to build on their perception of him as weak and scared. The thought made him want to laugh, but he kept it inside. He'd be laughing soon enough, and he was certain he'd be the only one.

They climbed the steps to the porch and stopped to wipe their feet before entering. The house smelled of freshly cut wood, but it came as no surprise. From what he could see, the woodwork was elaborate, the art of a true carpenter. It had been Cook's trade before his brother's death had spurred him down a radical's path.

"Father Cook?" Mike called out. "We have the boy, sir."

"Bring him downstairs," said a muffled voice from below.

Nate led the way down the short hallway and through the kitchen to a door in the far corner. Mike guided Tyler down the steep wooden stairs to the basement.

"It's us, Father," Nate said, as if Cook had forgotten they were coming.

"Be with you in a minute," Cook said as a table saw came to life, the whine of its rotating blade filling the basement workroom.

Tyler's eyes immediately took in his surroundings. Cook was directly across the room, his broad back to them as he worked at the saw. He seemed bigger, heavier than the dossier had reported.

He finished his work and switched off the machine. Smiling cheerfully, he turned around and removed his safety goggles. He had round features, pink cheeks, and salt-and-pepper hair worn in a buzz cut.

"Hello, there," he said, approaching Tyler with his hand outstretched.

Tyler couldn't respond.

"Take the restraints off," Cook ordered, then held out his large hand again.

Tyler took it weakly in his own.

"It's been a long time since I've seen you in the flesh, boy." Cook let his hand go and casually strolled toward another worktable, where an unassembled chair and some tools were resting. "Been a long time since me and your daddy talked as well."

Tyler rubbed at his wrists and lowered his head sadly. "The government came and took him."

Cook shook his head slowly, leaning his bulk against the worktable. "It's a sad day when our elected officials can persecute us for the friends we once kept, but this is just a sign of the times, I'm afraid."

From the corner of his eye Tyler could see Mike and Nate nodding in agreement.

"Me and your daddy used to talk about how the world was changing, moving further and further away from God and what our forefathers fought for." He picked up a chair leg from the table, hefting its weight in his large hand. "I told him I would change the world if I could," Cook said. "That I'd wake up the people of this great nation, make them see what's happening to their way of life right under their very noses."

Tyler cleared his throat nervously. "Daddy said that

you were a great man with great ideas and that the world could learn from you."

Cook smiled, still holding the chair leg in his left hand.

"Did your daddy really say that?" he asked, the pink in his cheeks growing darker.

"Yes, and he said that if anything ever happened to him, I was to come find you—which is exactly what I did."

The father of the brotherhood chuckled heartily and reached into his back pocket with his right hand. "You done good, boy," he said as he removed a folded piece of paper and tossed it to the ground in front of Tyler. "Pick it up."

Tyler reached down and grabbed the paper, unfolding it to reveal a photograph of a family in front of a Christmas tree. He recognized Ryan Childs at once, guessing that the woman and the boy in the picture were his wife and son. He also saw the problem—he didn't even come close to resembling Brady Childs; the kid was heavyset, with dark hair and evidence of a serious overbite.

"Got that with a card a while back; can't rightly think of the reason I saved it," Cook explained, a sneer twisting his friendly features. "But I'm sure glad I did."

Then he stepped quickly away from the worktable,

pulling his arm back and throwing the chair leg at Tyler's face.

Tyler watched the chair leg leave Cook's hand as if in slow motion, spinning through the air toward him. And at the precise moment he reached out and plucked it from the air before it could do him any harm.

He considered trying to explain why he no longer appeared the same as the boy in the Christmas photo but knew it would be useless. Besides, he was getting itchy.

It had already been nearly three months since his last kill.

It was like watching a movie—a very dark, violent movie.

Although the really scary thing was, he knew it was real. They were memories. They belonged to another, but they were leaking into his own thoughts—his own dreams.

Tom Lovett shared his mind with a killer. Tom Lovett *was* the killer, but then again, he wasn't. Pieces of the story cascaded through his thoughts, a bizarre set of footnotes, as this latest memory of violence unfolded before his mind's eye.

He wanted to look away, sensing the mayhem to come, but he was a captive audience, held in the unrelenting clutches of deep sleep.

Tom was just seventeen, but he was a teenager with a rare sleep disorder called Quentin's narcolepsy. It was a condition that caused him to fall asleep anytime, any-place, and not awaken until the spell had run its course. At least, that was what he'd always been told. The truth, he was finally learning, was even worse.

His focus returned to the violence. The killer's movements were a blur, the wooden post in his hand suddenly the deadliest of weapons. He lashed out first at Mike, behind him to the left, smashing the chair leg across the bridge of the man's nose. There was an explosion of brilliant crimson and Mike crumpled to the floor, clutching his face. Nate didn't even have a chance to react before the heavy piece of wood con-nected viciously with the side of his head. And as he fell backward to the floor, the killer hit him again for good measure.

Tom had recently discovered that his entire life had been a lie, perpetrated by the very people he had loved and trusted most. Tom Lovett wasn't just some teen with a rare sleep disorder—he was something alto-gether different.

Something deadly.

The Janus Project—a covert government program charged with creating the ultimate assassin—had used his condition and shaped him into something unlike anything the world had ever seen. A single body with two distinct personalities: one second a normal teenage boy, the next, a cold-blooded killer who would stop at nothing.

When a narcoleptic attack was triggered, Tom Lovett went away and the killer—Tyler Garrett—was awakened.

Tyler was fast, but not fast enough. Cook had charged, and as the killer turned to meet his attack, the large man tackled him. They crashed backward into a series of cabinets, thrashing on the concrete floor as screws, nails, and loose tools rained down on them.

Cook appeared to be dominating, but then Tyler managed to raise his arms, smacking both hands flat against the sides of the man's head.

Tom could hear Cook's piercing scream as his eardrums were ruptured. He wanted to wake up; he knew how it would end; it always ended the same.

With murder.

And that was how it had almost ended for him as well. The Janus Project had wanted him dead, but he hadn't wanted to die, and neither had the personality who shared his mind. And so the two had begun to merge. Tom had so far managed to maintain his dominance, but Tyler's murderous persona was gradually leaking into his waking life. Almost every day he had begun to notice subtle changes in himself—knowledge of weapons he'd never seen, fighting techniques he'd never studied, violent, aggressive reactions to certain situations.

And the dreams—the disturbing memories that were slowly becoming part of his own.

The killer sprang to his feet and dove across the workroom, but Cook moved quickly as well, grabbing hold of his ankle, causing him to stumble. Cook was on his feet in a flash, twin trickles of blood trailing from both ears, the curved blade of a carpet knife suddenly in his hand.

Tyler snatched up a stray piece of pine from the ground, using it to shield his chest just as the knife slashed across him. He lashed out with the piece of wood, the corner catching Cook's arm, knocking the knife from his grasp. He jumped to his feet, driving the palm of his hand up under the man's chin—a blow that would have rendered any ordinary man unconscious.

But it appeared that Elijah Cook was far from an ordinary man. He stumbled back a step, his eyes flickering as he seemed to fight with passing out, but less than a second later he had fully recovered, bringing his own fist down on the killer. Tyler managed to block the blow, but its force was so great that it drove him back. Again he lost his footing and began to stumble.

Tom could feel Tyler's emotions—while Tom was afraid, he could sense Tyler's unbridled excitement at the same time. This was what he lived for, what he had been born to do.

As he stumbled, Tyler twisted to the side and fell against the table with the power saw. Next to the machine were the spare blades. Without a moment's hesitation he snatched one up and spun around, letting the blade fly at its target, a murderous Frisbee.

Cook had retrieved Mike's shotgun and was just aiming down its barrel when the spinning saw blade plunged into the soft flesh of his neck. The shotgun erupted as he dropped it and stumbled backward, desperately clawing at the blade in his throat.

The stray blasts ignited cans of paint thinner that had been stacked in the corner near the workstation. There was a fiery explosion, and the cellar became filled with choking fumes and fire. Tyler moved quickly through the smoke, avoiding the spreading flames, using pure instinct to navigate the blinding fog.

And as he climbed the stairs to safety, Tom struggled with the overpowering sense of helplessness and fear that he felt every time he was forced to experience one of Tyler's murderous memories. It was a fear unlike anything he had known before, the fear that at some point his guard would come down and the killer lurking in the shadows of his mind would grab the opportunity.

The opportunity to take control.

Forever.

"Tom, are you all right?"

Tom recognized the voice as Christian Tremain's, coming from a speaker hidden somewhere in the room. He sat up in his bed, his body drenched with sweat.

"M'fine," he mumbled, running his hands through his sandy blond hair, trying to push the violent images from his mind.

"Hypnagogic attack?" Tremain asked, referring to the bizarre hallucinations that were a symptom of Tom's sleep disorder.

"No," Tom said, now searching the plain white room for a camera as well. "Didn't realize I was being watched."

Tremain made a noise that could have been a chuckle. "You're the product of an experiment to create the ultimate assassin. Of course you're being watched."

Tom shuddered. He hated being thought of as an experiment created in a lab—images from countless old Frankenstein movies ran through his head.

But at least Tremain was one of the good guys, or so he claimed. He was the director of the Pandora Group. The Janus Project and its director, Brandon Kavanagh, were once part of that agency, but Kavanagh had broken off on his own and was now trying to sell the sleeper technology to the highest bidder. Tom had never seen Kavanagh, but he was certain his other half had, and he was waiting for the day when the memory would be shared and he could see the face of the man who had taken so much from him—the face of the man he was going to kill.

Tom tossed the covers back and got up; he couldn't shake Tyler's latest memory. He kept seeing the faces of the dead men, and as he thought of them, a slight tremble of excitement went through his body.

The thrill of the kill.

"I remembered another one of his . . ." Tom paused, not really sure what he would call it. "Assignments?" He sat back down on the side of the bed, suddenly exhausted.

"What was it this time?" Tremain asked. "Another assassination?"

Tom nodded. "Some guy named Cook—in Virginia."

"Founder of the Brotherhood of the New Dawn. I remember. He died in a mysterious fire that practically burned down his entire compound."

"Mysterious." Tom laughed nervously.

"The FBI went in after the explosions."

"Explosions?"

"Yep, besides the stuff that went up in the fire, the agents found a hidden cache of high explosives— enough to cause catastrophic damage to, say, a federal office building."

Tom placed his face in his hands. "So he actually was a bad guy," he said with a hint of relief.

"This one was, yes," Tremain replied.

The image of a kindly, gray-haired old man dressed in baggy pants and a heavy sweater suddenly appeared in Tom's mind. The man was sitting in a beat-up old chair in a cabin, happily puffing on a pipe. Tom preferred to remember Dr. Bernard Quentin this way rather than the other, on the floor of the same cabin, three bullet holes in his chest.

Dr. Quentin had discovered the rare sleep disorder that bore his name, and it was his research that Kavanagh and company had exploited to create the sleeper agents. Quentin had known early on that his studies were being corrupted, and so he'd devised a way to stop Kavanagh—a way to use one of Kavanagh's own assassins against him. He'd planted a secret message within the mind of a test subject, a fail-safe mechanism that, on Quentin's murder, would trigger realizations in the sleeper subject of who he really was and what he was being used to do.

Tom was that test subject, and as the truth had been

revealed to him, his entire life had crumbled. Even the couple he'd thought were his parents had turned out to be nothing more than handlers in Kavanagh's employ, keeping him healthy and safe until a killer was needed and a switch was flipped to make Tom go away.

Well, thanks to Quentin, Tom wasn't going anywhere anymore.

"It's still pretty early." Tremain's voice filtered through the speaker, forcing him from his reverie. "Why don't you try to get some more sleep?"

Thinking about his situation had left Tom restless, and he stood up from the bed.

"I'm done with sleep."

Agent Abernathy's fist connected with the side of Tom's face, snapping his head violently to the right. Tom's mouth was suddenly filled with the coppery taste of blood and his ears rang loudly. He stumbled back away from his assailant.

"I don't understand how kicking my ass is going to help anything," he complained as he removed the padded headgear and looked to Tremain, who stood on the sidelines of the workout room, sipping coffee from a plastic cup.

"We need to see how much of the Tyler persona has been assimilated into your own," he said. "And if new information can be accessed when it's needed."

Tom shook his head. He was tired of all the testing and prodding that had become his life since arriving at the Pandora facility. "You already know what I can do," he said, exasperation creeping into his voice.

Tremain had been there the day Tom had survived the attack by a Janus assault squad and his own parents.

Tom felt his rage surge. No, those people weren't his parents—they never had been, and the sooner he accepted that, the better off he'd be. No matter how many times he thought about their betrayal, he couldn't bring himself to let them go. There were still so many good memories.

But then, those were likely lies as well, implants, false memories to make him believe his life was real.

All so they could hide a killer inside his head.

Tremain took another sip of his coffee as two more agents dressed in workout gear entered the gym and joined Abernathy.

"Humor us, Tom," Tremain said. "Just spar with them. They won't hurt you."

Abernathy grinned and winked at Tom as he slowly approached the three agents.

"It's not me that I'm worried about," Tom grumbled, placing the padded gear back on his head.

"So how do you want to do this?" he asked, standing in front of the men, focusing his attention on Agent Abernathy. "Want to crack me in the face again to remind me where we left off?"

The man laughed. "That was just a love tap, kid,"

he said, punching the knuckles of his red padded gloves together. "Thought you were something special—guess I was wrong."

The other agents chuckled, and Tom felt something within him snap. Abernathy didn't even see it coming. Tom reacted instantaneously, smashing his fist across the agent's handsome, grinning face. He stumbled back toward his buddies, who caught him and saved him from falling.

Tom punched his own gloved fists together, imitating Abernathy. "Special enough to kick your ass, I guess," he said.

Abernathy recovered fast, shaking off the punch and coming at Tom straight on, fists raised to give him the beating of his life.

Tom had planted his feet and was waiting for that spark of inspiration that would show him how to react when he heard Tremain yell from the sidelines.

"All of you, take him down—hard, if you have to."

Tom shot him a quick, surprised glance, and Tremain raised his coffee cup in a mock salute. Tom turned back to the three agents in time to see Abernathy's fist careening toward his face, and suddenly his brain somehow slowed down the action. He moved his head from the path of the punch, feeling a breeze as the leather-clad fist sailed past, dangerously close.

Then Tom stepped in, grabbing hold of Abernathy's arm at the elbow, bending it sharply in a direction it wasn't meant to go. He heard the agent hiss in pain and applied even more pressure, forcing him to choose between a broken arm or dropping to his knees.

"What's it gonna be?" Tom asked, feeling the man begin to struggle, but then common sense prevailed, and Abernathy lowered himself to the floor.

Tom pushed the man away and turned to the other two agents, who now circled him. He didn't know their names, but he had seen them around the Pandora facility. They were stereotypical special agents—square-jawed, painfully serious, and in excellent physical condition.

Just two more pieces of meat that need to be cut down to size, he thought with a weird tingle of fear and excitement as he attacked his opponents, not a doubt in his mind that he would soon be the only one standing.

Well, I'll be damned, Tremain thought, drinking from his cup, afraid that if he took his eyes from the scene, he just might miss something.

Deacons and Stanley attacked together, and if Tremain had been a betting man, he wouldn't have given a second thought to who the victors of this little rumble would be. After all, a kid, weighing, what, one-twenty, one-thirty at the absolute most, shouldn't have stood a chance against two former CIA operatives.

The kid moved like a blur, taking out Stanley—the larger of the two agents—first. He seemed to defy gravity as he leapt into the air to deliver a spinning kick that nearly took the agent's head off. Tremain thought that Deacons might have gained the upper hand when he grabbed Tom from behind and pinned the kid's arms to his sides. But the advantage was only temporary.

Tom was able to squirm around in the agent's grasp; then he drove his forehead into the man's chin, forcing him to lose his grip.

Tremain felt the chill of dread at the base of his neck. The boy was smiling as he delivered an open-palm strike to the center of Deacons's chest. The man stumbled back, gasping for breath, and fell to the floor.

That wasn't a challenge for him at all, Tremain realized. There could have been four more agents in the room and he doubted it would have mattered. The kid hadn't even broken a sweat. But that was what Tremain needed to see. He had to know how much of Tyler Garrett had been absorbed into Tom's psyche. And maybe—just maybe—he could access the information that would lead them to Kavanagh.

Tom was standing in the center of the gym, his head

slowly moving from side to side as he sized up his adversaries. The three Pandora agents were gradually recovering, slowly rising to their feet, looking a bit rough around the edges.

"Is that all you've got?" he heard Tom ask them, swaying gently. His eyes darted between each of the agents, recording their every movement as he readied himself to spring into action.

Fascinating, Tremain caught himself thinking as he watched the boy. He immediately stifled his admiration; these skills had been created by Kavanagh for the sake of greed and destruction.

The agents had given up, raising their hands in a sign of submission as they began to walk away. Tremain, believing the session to be over, headed for a nearby trash can to dispose of his empty cup. The sounds of violence distracted him, and he turned back to the center of the room, stunned to find Tom attacking the agents with abandon.

Deacons lay on the ground, unmoving, blood from his mouth and nose forming a puddle beneath his head.

Stanley was attempting to get away, running in a crouch toward the exit, but Tom was right behind him—a predator on the hunt. With what appeared to be little effort, Tom sprang into the air, propelling himself toward the back of the fleeing agent. The heel of his sneaker connected with the back of Stanley's head, sending him sprawling, unconscious, to the floor.

"Tom! Stop!" Tremain hollered, but the boy didn't seem to hear.

He was already moving toward Abernathy, the last of his adversaries. The agent was standing, ready for the attack, and there was fear in the seasoned veteran's eyes.

"Tom, stop this right now! They've had enough!"

Tom sprang at Abernathy, raining a flurry of blows on his face. The Pandora agent was driven to his knees under the relentless onslaught, his hands trying to protect his bloody face. Tom grabbed him by the hair, pulling back his head, preparing to deliver a blow to the man's throat.

A killing strike.

Slowly Tremain approached them. "Tom," he said quietly, and again there was no response.

"Tyler, stand down!" the director suddenly bellowed, his voice echoing around the gymnasium.

The boy let Abernathy's limp body drop to the floor. He glared at Tremain, and for a moment the director felt like he was in the presence of someone else entirely.

"My name is Tom," the boy said through gritted teeth, then turned on his heels and stormed from the gym.

But as Tremain stared at his three fallen agents, he had to wonder if that was altogether true.

Madison Fitzgerald was leaving the Pandora Group, returning to her mother's home in Chicago.

She didn't have much to pack, certainly not enough to warrant the large duffel bag they had given her. *A shopping bag would have been more than enough,* she thought, double-checking the dresser drawers. Most of the things she'd had at her aunt and uncle's house had been lost in the explosion that had destroyed their home as well as the Lovetts' next door—*or whoever the hell they were.*

Madison felt a twinge of lingering fear as she thought about how she'd almost died.

She went through the bag resting on her bed in an attempt to distract herself—a few T-shirts, jeans, some sweatpants, mostly provided by the Pandora Group.

Her aunt and uncle had been brought here too, but they'd quickly been relocated. Along with her parents, they'd been fed a story about Tom's family being part of some radical anti-government group planning terrorist acts and told that the explosions had been caused by bomb-making equipment stored in their basement. They'd all bought it, but Madison knew otherwise. The truth was still so hard to process, though . . . the fact that she'd fallen for someone harder than she'd ever fallen before. And that someone, Tom, happened to have a second personality who was a cold-blooded killer.

She shook the thought from her mind and went to the bathroom to get her soap and shampoo. Catching a glimpse of herself in the mirror over the sink, she stopped, staring at her reflection. Before all this her biggest problem had been her parents' divorce. It almost felt like she wasn't even the same person anymore. Madison stuffed her shampoo into the duffel with her clothes and sighed, sitting down heavily on the bed.

Just that morning she'd gone through something called a debriefing. She'd sat at a table and been given page after page of documents to sign, each of them telling her what she could and couldn't talk about to the outside world unless she wanted to spend some time in jail.

Who would believe me anyway? she wondered, zipping the bag closed.

Madison looked at the clock on the dresser and saw that it was almost noon. They'd be coming soon to drive her to the airport, the beginning of her journey home.

Home.

Her mind raced. Was it possible to go back to a

normal life? Did she even want to? But what choice did she have—they certainly wouldn't let her hang around the Pandora Group.

The digital clock flashed 12:00, and she stood, grabbing her bag and slinging it over her shoulder. She was surprised that no one had arrived at her door. She'd sort of been expecting Tom.

She crossed the room, trying not to think about why he hadn't come to say goodbye. Just as she reached for the knob, there was a knock. She opened the door and found herself looking into Tom Lovett's gorgeous eyes. His hair was wild, his cheeks flushed.

"Thank God you're still here," he said, slightly out of breath. "I was in the gym—lost track of the time. I was afraid I was gonna miss you."

He smiled at her then, and she had no choice but to smile back.

How could she ever live without Tom Lovett?

Tom leaned against the door frame and sighed with relief. She was still here.

"When I saw the time, I started to freak—"

"I would've waited," she interrupted, slipping her hands into the back pockets of her jeans.

He smiled. *God, she's beautiful.* It still knocked him out every time he saw her.

"So you're going, huh?" he said, silently cursing himself for sounding lame.

Madison nodded. "Back to the old homestead," she said, avoiding his eyes. "Mom's still there, but Dad moved out a couple of months ago."

"It must be sort of weird, so much has changed," Tom said.

"Yeah, but it'll still be home. I guess that's lucky."

Tom secretly envied her at that moment, having something to return to. Everything he had known—his past, his home, and family, everything that had defined him as a person—was gone.

Everything except Madison, and now . . .

"So are they going to keep you here?" she asked, her striking green eyes finally meeting his.

Tom shrugged. "I guess. They want to do more tests and stuff."

"Guess they got what they needed from me," she said, smiling sadly.

"You shouldn't be here anyway," he told her, shaking his head. "This isn't the place for you."

"It isn't for you either," Madison said. "I'm worried about you."

He smiled. "Don't be. I'll be fine. There's still a lot I have to learn about myself and about what's been done to me."

"I just feel bad about leaving you," she repeated, again refusing to look at him. "We've been through so much."

Tom swallowed, his heart racing. All he wanted to do was hold her, bring her close, kiss her the way he'd wanted to since the first time he'd seen her. There'd just been so much happening, and then here at the facility, there were always the guards around. . . . His gaze flicked out to the hallway, and he saw it was clear. He stepped forward, about to reach out to her, when Madison suddenly turned and ducked back inside her room. He stood in the doorway, watching as she went to the bedside table and opened the drawer. She removed a pad of paper and a pen and began to write.

"Here," she said, handing him the folded piece of paper.

"What's this?" he asked, before opening it.

"My e-mail address and phone number," she answered.

"Cool." He read the address, already committing it to memory. "They haven't given me e-mail access yet—"

"Well, as soon as you get it, write to me," she finished for him.

He noticed that she was looking at something over his shoulder and turned to see a Pandora agent standing there, waiting.

"Looks like your escort has arrived," he said quietly, disappointment knotting in his stomach.

"Looks that way." She reached down to pick up her bag.

Tom felt a wave of panic. He didn't want her to leave—didn't want to say goodbye to his only comfort.

The agent glanced at his watch. "You really need to go," Tom said, trying to sound nonchalant. "You don't want to miss your flight."

Madison looked over to her escort and held up a finger asking for one more minute. The man nodded but only took a couple of steps aside, still watching them.

"This is it," she said, and all Tom could do was nod stiffly as he wrestled with emotions he could barely contain.

She dropped the bag to the floor and threw her arms around him in a hug. Tom wrapped his own arms around her, holding her tightly. Her body melted into his.

"You take care of yourself, Tom Lovett," Madison whispered against his neck, her voice shaking with emotion.

Tom took a deep breath and gently pushed her away. "You'd better get going." He inclined his head toward the guard. "He's waiting."

Madison kept her hands clasped around his neck, and he stared into her bright green eyes for another moment. His eyes traveled down to her lips, and again he thought about kissing her, not even caring anymore about the guard standing there. But he hesitated, and suddenly she was picking up her bag and, without another word, walking away.

Tom watched as she turned the corner with the guard, feeling more empty and alone than ever.

CHAPTER 3

"Brandon. What kind a sissy name is that?" the older boy asked as he cast his fishing line into the pond.

"It was my granddaddy's."

"Was your granddaddy a sissy too?"

Brandon felt a surge of anger. He dropped his home-made fishing pole and clutched his fists to his sides. "You take that back," he demanded.

"Make me." A disturbing smile spread across the bully's face as he stepped closer.

"You ain't worth piss." Brandon dismissed him with the words he'd heard his grandmother use on the hired help and bent down to retrieve his fishing pole.

But it didn't end there.

Brandon Kavanagh suddenly opened his eyes. He was disoriented as he looked around the office. But quickly his mind threw off the sluggishness of sleep, and he remembered exactly where he was and how he had come to be there.

He was a wanted man, and the thought made him smile. *It's sort of exciting being on the other side,* he thought as he stretched his arms above his head. He stood and headed for the coffee machine in the corner, a little caffeine to clear away the cobwebs.

Kavanagh filled a ceramic mug with the steaming black liquid, carefully taking a sip and wrinkling his nose at the bitter taste. He missed his former secretary—Karen. She'd made the best coffee.

The image of the pretty older woman slumped over her desk, body riddled with bullet holes, filled his mind. Pandora had wanted him—wanted him badly. He sipped his coffee, remembering the sound of gunfire in the Janus Project's West Virginia facility. They would have killed him if he hadn't been prepared.

He'd always known what it would mean to attempt to profit from the information gleaned from Janus, but Kavanagh didn't care. He'd seen too much of this nasty old world to hold the concept of good or evil in any high regard.

It was all shades of gray to him.

All that mattered was staying on top. He'd learned

that as a child. The lesson taking the form of a bully's pounding fists.

He chuckled as he returned to his desk, careful not to spill the contents of his cup. It had been years since Kavanagh had had a conscious thought of the boy who had set him on the path to being the man he was today. He reached up to touch the bump of scar tissue on his scalp and remembered how heavily he had bled.

Hit with my own fishing pole, he recalled. *Probably should have gotten stitches, but Grandma didn't agree, and what Grandma said went.*

Miserable old witch.

The door buzzer sounded, pulling him from his reverie, and he looked at a small monitor by his desk to see who it was.

"Come in, Noah," Kavanagh said into the intercom, pushing the button to unlock the heavy metal door.

His personal assistant and head of security stepped into the new office space and stopped to look around. "Love what you've done with the place," he said with sarcasm as he helped himself to a cup of coffee.

"Just goes to show you the versatility of an abandoned underground military base," Kavanagh said with equal derision. "I'm not going to be happy until every room in the place looks this good."

Wells sipped his coffee and made a face. "It's times

like these that I really miss Karen," he said as he took a seat in one of the chairs in front of Kavanagh's desk.

"Tell me about it," Kavanagh replied, watching the man set the cup down on the edge of his desk. "So, what's the good word?"

He had sent Wells to check on the results of an auction that was on the verge of coming to a close. What corrupt third world power or terrorist organization wouldn't give their eyeteeth for technology that created the ultimate killing machine? Wells picked at specks of lint on his pants and said nothing.

"That's not very encouraging, Noah," Kavanagh said, feeling his ire on the rise.

"The auction fell apart." Wells slowly made eye contact.

"What the hell do you mean, it fell apart?" Kavanagh growled.

"The bids were retracted," Wells explained. "Evidently the word is out on our problems with Pandora." He shrugged. "Some of them think we're too hot; they're doubting our ability to deliver."

Kavanagh seethed. After he'd resigned as director of acquisitions, the Janus Project had been his primary focus: taking the idea of creating the ultimate sleeper agent and nurturing it slowly, painfully to fruition. The fact that somebody—especially some two-bit dictator with delusions of grandeur—doubted his ability was almost enough to make him to want to walk away.

Almost.

"So where are we now?" Kavanagh asked, trying to remain calm.

Wells shrugged again. "Nowhere, really. They've all crawled back to their holes, waiting to see how this plays out."

Kavanagh laughed, leaning back in his chair and looking up at the huge vent in the ceiling. The stale, recirculated air of the underground facility blew on his face. "What do they mean, how this plays out? Either they want the product or they don't. It's as simple as that."

Noah plucked a silver cigarette lighter from his pocket and flipped it open. "I think they want proof," he said, idly holding his index finger in the hungry flame. "I think they want to see that we're not afraid—but that's just my take." The faint stink of burning flesh filled the air.

Noah Wells had first come to Kavanagh's attention as part of another Pandora project called, aptly enough— Invincible. The former navy SEAL had been a volunteer, subjecting himself to experimentation that deadened the small nerve fibers that carry sensations of pain, heat, and cold to the body. Invincible had been attempting to create a soldier incapable of feeling pain, thus making him more effective on the battlefield. There'd been some successes, like Noah Wells. But there had also been side effects: some of the drugs being used had incited violent and masochistic tendencies in the test subjects. Invincible had eventually been shut down to make way for more promising projects, like Janus.

Kavanagh had made it a point to seek out Wells, believing him to be the perfect choice for the job he'd had in mind, and he'd been right. It was like having a really smart pit bull, and the fact that Wells no longer had the capacity to feel pain was an added bonus.

"Do you mind?" Kavanagh asked.

"Sorry." Wells flicked the lid of the lighter closed and placed it back in his pocket.

Kavanagh turned his chair to the wall, signaling the end of their meeting. He had a lot to think about. Wells rose, finishing his coffee in one long gulp before walking to the door.

"Wells?" Kavanagh called as he pulled open the heavy door.

"Sir?"

"Have the doc look at that burn on your finger, would you? Wouldn't want it to get infected."

Tom lay on his bed, looking up at the ceiling, smirking to himself. *A kid with narcolepsy who can't sleep; if it wasn't so friggin' pathetic, it'd be funny.*

He'd been tossing and turning for hours, his thoughts racing. He already missed Madison and could have kicked himself for not kissing her before she left. Guard or no guard, it had been the perfect chance. And what if it had been his only chance?

He thought about how he had reacted during Tremain's exercise. At first it had been all about showing those guys that he was more than something to be laughed at. But then it had gotten serious.

Deadly serious.

Tom felt himself break out in a cold, tingling sweat, wondering for the thousandth time if he would have actually killed Abernathy if Tremain hadn't intervened. But what he found equally disturbing was his own reaction to Tyler's name.

Who am I really? he wondered. Tom had believed he knew the answer to that question, but the more he thought about it, the harder it was becoming for him to give an honest answer.

And that frightened him.

Something was wrong, even more so than before. Tom was still finding it difficult to maintain control. Aspects of the Tyler personality that he'd thought were safely absorbed into his own persona were becoming harder and harder to manage. Tom wished there was some way he could communicate with his other half, but besides the dreams, Tyler had been strangely silent, hiding in some dark corner of his brain, waiting for who knew what.

Tom sat up, looking at the ceiling. He knew a camera must be up there. "Hello?" he said, waving. "Anybody there?"

He got no answer. Maybe they'd decided not to watch him tonight, he thought, bolting from his bed and going to the door.

A sentry stationed at a small desk in the hallway looked up from his paperback, alarm in his eyes.

The Pandora Group was partially responsible for the technology that had done this to him. It only made sense that they would be the ones to help him figure it out.

A few days ago they'd asked him to participate in some tests that would determine the extent of the assimilation of his two personalities, and he had outright refused, sick of feeling like a guinea pig. Now Tom figured it might be in his best interests to be more cooperative.

"I need to speak to Tremain," he told the guard.

The man checked his watch before giving him a quizzical look.

"I know it's late, but tell him that I agree," he told the man, certain that this was the right decision.

"Tell him that I'll participate in his tests."

Madison was surprised by how unremarkable it all seemed to her now. She was back where she had so badly wanted to be, only to find that it wasn't half as interesting as where she had been.

She missed Tom already.

"Your father is meeting us at the house," her mother said, her eyes on the road as she drove.

Madison said nothing, looking out the window at the passing traffic, remembering the last time she'd been on this road—on the way to Massachusetts to live with Uncle Marty and Aunt Ellen.

"We're so grateful you're safe," her mother tried again, and then sniffled.

Madison glanced at her and saw that she was crying.

Both of her parents had been ready to jump on a plane to Washington when they'd heard about what happened, but Pandora had been able to convince them otherwise. Instead, she had spoken to them by phone every night just to prove that she was okay, and then after multiple debriefings, an exit interview, and a ride on a private jet, here she was.

Right back where she had started.

"Hey, what are the tears for?" She reached across the seat to rest a comforting hand on her mother's shoulder. "I'm all right."

If she only knew the truth. *How many times was my life actually threatened?* Madison wondered, feeling an unpleasant roiling in the pit of her belly.

Her mother smiled, quickly glancing in Madison's direction before returning her eyes to the road. Her cheeks were stained with tears.

"I'm sorry, it's just that with everything that's been going on . . ."

With everything that's been going on, Madison thought, knowing her mother meant the divorce. She hated to think that when she finally got home, nothing would be the same, but no amount of obsessing was going to change anything. Besides, everybody was alive and safe, and wasn't that more important?

"I get it," she said, giving her mother's shoulder a squeeze. "But I really am fine. Quit worrying."

Her mother smiled briefly and went on to talk about

Marty and Ellen, who were living with Marty's brother in Connecticut until their home could be rebuilt. "It was a blessing that no one was hurt," she said, and her eyes again welled with emotion.

No one who mattered to you, Madison thought, thinking of Tom's parents—or whoever they really were. No remains had ever been found in the wreckage of the two homes, and she had to wonder, *Could anybody have actually survived an explosion like that?*

Madison turned to the window again. They were getting closer to home, but she it was barely registering the familiar neighborhood. She was thinking about Tom again, pictures from the last few weeks flashing in her mind. She saw him taking on three armed soldiers, the memory blurring into the vicious fight he'd had with the man posing as his father. Madison felt her cheeks flush at the memory.

"Madison, are you listening?" her mother asked.

"Sorry," Madison said, realizing she'd been tuning her out.

"Is there anything you need? We could stop at the store before—"

"I'm fine. Let's just get home. I can always go out again later."

They pulled into the driveway, and she saw her father's car parked over to the side. She smiled, feeling her heartbeat quicken. It had been months since she'd last seen him.

From the corner of her eye she saw her mother's pained expression as he came out the front door and down the front steps to greet her. There were lots of hugs and kisses for her, but her parents didn't speak, as if they had somehow become invisible to each other.

They helped her with her things, escorting her into the house, and Madison was surprised, despite all her conflicting feelings, at how good it actually felt—how comforting it was to be back in her own house. She walked around the first floor, readjusting herself to her surroundings, noticing everything her father had taken when he left.

She was on her way to the kitchen from the den when she heard them—harsh whispers as the two fought about something. She sighed and leaned against the wall of the hallway, fighting back tears. *Welcome home! Yeah, right.*

She took a deep breath and headed down the hall, hearing the heated discussion come to an abrupt end as she neared the kitchen. "I'm going to my room for a while," she called out as she passed, doing her best to keep her voice steady.

For a moment she thought they might argue, but they left her alone. She closed the door behind her and looked around. She was comforted by the sight of her old room.

She lay down on her bed, snuggling into the familiar mattress, and snatched up an old stuffed bear that she'd had since first grade. She gazed at the ceiling, hugging the stuffed animal to her chest, her thoughts already returning to Tom.

She wondered what he was doing. She wondered if he was thinking about her.

The room smelled of antiseptic and seemed to be much colder than it should have been.

Tom lay on the exam table, gazing up at the tiled ceiling, listening as the lab techs readied their elaborate tests. All he could think about was the sight of Madison walking away from him before he could kiss her. *If only she hadn't had to leave.*

When they'd first arrived at the Pandora facility, Tom and Madison had insisted on being together at all times, watching each other's backs. He imagined he would be a lot less nervous if she was here now as well.

He turned his head to the door as it opened. Christian Tremain came inside. As always, the director of the Pandora Group looked like he'd slept in his clothes, shirt-tails untucked, red-and-blue-striped tie slightly askew.

"How are we doing?" he asked, placing his hand on

Tom's arm. "You still okay with this? All you have to do is say the word. I don't want to force you into anything—"

"I'm fine," Tom interrupted. "I wouldn't have agreed if I didn't want to do it."

Tremain nodded and looked around the lab. "Dr. Stempler?" he called, and Tom heard the buzz of conversation from somewhere across the room suddenly stop.

"Would you give Tom a rundown as to what we're attempting to do today?"

Tom sat up on the table as a short, stocky man in a stained lab coat, with a shiny bald head and thick circular glasses, approached. He was sweating profusely, even in the room's frigid temperature, and Tom couldn't help but think about the stereotypical mad scientist. He held out his hand to shake, but the man simply stared at it as though it was filthy.

"Yes," Stempler said, in a high-pitched, nasal voice. "Today we're going to attempt to make contact with the persona sharing your brain."

His eyes were cold and unblinking, and Tom didn't like the way they made him feel, sort of like a bug under a microscope.

"How are you going to do that?" Tom asked. "I've been trying for days without a peep."

Stempler motioned to one of his techs. The man obliged by carrying over a thick folder, which the scientist proceeded to leaf through—completely ignoring Tom's question.

"The boy asked you a question, Doctor," Tremain stated.

The scientist slowly looked up, fixing the director with a similar icy stare. Tremain met the look with a special gaze all his own, and Tom could almost feel the tension between the two men.

Stempler sighed, removed his thick glasses, and rubbed at his eyes. "Very well. According to your file, you mention a location within your subconscious." He placed his glasses back on his face and opened the folder again. His mouth moved silently as he read. "A run-down structure—a mansion is how you described it," he said, looking up.

"Yeah," Tom said. "He was inside waiting for me. He said it was a place of his own creation."

"Exactly," Stempler continued. "And we think he might be hiding there."

"That's all well and good," Tom said, "but I have no idea how to get back there. The first time was a total fluke, something to do with the code Dr. Quentin—"

"Yes, yes, we know, and that is why I am here," Stempler interrupted with an air of self-importance.

"Dr. Stempler is our resident expert on the subconscious and memory retrieval," Tremain explained. "In fact, some of his research was used by Janus when implanting Tyler within your psyche."

Tom felt a cold anger twist inside him. "Great, so you're one of the people I should thank," he said through gritted teeth.

Stempler smiled, oblivious to the sarcasm. "Using a combination of hypnotism and a drug developed to help treat multiple personality disorder, we're hoping to place you deep within your mind, peeling away the layers of your subconscious like an onion so that you will find the mansion again and hopefully the other half of your elusive dual personality."

Tom stiffened. The idea of being pumped full of drugs, helpless and at the whim of the Pandora's scientists, didn't leave him with a very good feeling.

"Remember what I said earlier, Tom," Tremain reminded.

But deep down Tom knew this was necessary: if there was a chance for him to help himself and to help Pandora locate Kavanagh before he had the chance to do any more harm, now was the time to do it.

"I'm fine," he said with a determined nod, lying back down on the table. "Let's do it."

Tremain stepped back, allowing the team of technicians to get at the boy. He looked frightened as one

tech swabbed his arm, preparing to insert an intra-
venous needle, while others attached circular, sticky
pads to his chest, wires trailing back to an EKG
machine.

It's all for his own good, Tremain kept telling himself,
but he knew that his real reason for doing this was to
locate Kavanagh. He made eye contact with the boy,
and Tom slowly raised his hand, giving him a thumbs-
up. Tremain smiled, realizing he'd started to care about
this kid who—at the flick of a switch—could be trans-
formed into one of the deadliest of killers. He hoped
that Pandora would eventually be able to do something
for Tom, to make his life as normal as possible. But
recalling the scene in the workout room the morning
before, Tremain wasn't so sure.

"How are we doing here, Doc?" he asked, strolling
over to stand beside Stempler.

The scientist was sitting behind a control panel, his
chubby fingers moving over the dials, knobs, and
switches. "Almost ready."

Tremain glanced back at Tom and saw that a head-
piece resembling a bike helmet was being affixed to the
boy's head.

"What's this for?" he heard Tom ask, but no one
offered an answer.

"Tell him," Tremain barked. It frustrated him that

the scientists were treating the boy as if he were nothing more than a lab rat.

Stempler exhaled in exasperation. "The helmet will stimulate REM sleep, quickly moving you through the other four stages to the deepest level of your subconscious, where we believe your other personality is hiding. Any more questions?"

Tom looked a little stunned as he attempted to digest the information.

"Good." The scientist returned to his digital readouts. "Satisfied?" he shot over his shoulder at Tremain.

The director felt his blood pressure spike. "You know, it's rather funny," he said with a humorless chuckle. "But I get the impression that you think I'm working for you."

Stempler looked up from the control panel, his beady eyes wide.

"Let me set you straight, Doctor." Tremain moved menacingly closer, pleased when everyone in the lab froze where they stood.

"You take orders from me. And I say Tom Lovett is to be treated the way you'd want your own mother to be treated here. If I see otherwise, we'll continue this discussion in private."

Tremain fell silent, folding his hands behind his back, letting the technicians and doctors get back to work.

Tom leaned past the tech who was now inserting the IV into his arm and smirked at him.

"We're ready to begin," Stempler said, looking to Tremain for approval.

"Thank you, Doctor," Tremain stated with authority. "Did you hear that, Tom?"

"Heard it," Tom replied.

"And are you ready?"

"As ready as I'm ever going to be," Tom slurred, the drug already starting to take effect.

It was different than one of his narcoleptic attacks.

The medication made him feel groggy and the helmet on his head made his brain tingle. It wasn't long before Tom found himself gradually slipping down into unconsciousness.

"Is everything all right, Tom?" he heard Stempler's voice ask from the darkness.

"Where are you?" Tom asked.

"I'm here in the lab," he explained. "I'm going to accompany you on the journey to your subconscious. I want you to tell me everything that you see and hear while you're there. Do you understand, Tom?"

The sensation of falling had increased, and for a moment he wondered if he would be hurt when he finally hit bottom.

"Do you understand, Tom?" Stempler repeated.

"Got it," Tom said, distracted momentarily from his worry. He'd been here before, but never had he been so aware.

It's like being in the deepest part of the ocean, he thought, continuing to descend. *Where the light of the sun can't reach me.*

He lost all concept of time and seemed to be falling for days, but he knew that had to be impossible.

Didn't it?

"Where are you now, Tom?" the doctor suddenly asked, startling him.

"I'm still falling," he said, before he realized he had stopped.

Now he stood on a rocky pathway, at the end of which was a house—no, a mansion, one that he had seen before.

"I'm here," he said softly. "I found it."

"Excellent," Stempler responded. "What do you see?"

Tom started to walk down the path toward the structure; it was twilight within his psyche, and he had to squint through the shadows to see. "It's different," he said as he moved closer.

There was something around the house—something had wrapped itself around the old structure.

"Vines," Tom explained, moving closer for a better look. "Thick, giant vines encircling the entire house, and they're covered with thorns."

"It appears that the alternate personality has set up a perimeter defense to prevent you from reaching him."

Tom laid his hand on one of the thick growths; it felt warm.

"Do you see any way past the vines, Tom?" the doctor asked.

At first he didn't, but on closer examination, he saw that there might actually be a way through.

"It'll be a tight fit," he said, bending down to peer through the opening that seemed to lead into the heart of the thicket. "But I think I can do it."

"Then I suggest you do so."

It was indeed a tight fit, but he squeezed himself into the opening, careful to avoid being pricked by the nasty-looking thorns. It was slow going as he made his way deeper.

"How are we doing, Tom?" Stempler asked, and Tom wished he would leave him alone.

He had reached a very narrow spot, an opening that he thought he could fit through proving to be smaller than he had expected.

"What's happening, Tom?"

"Leave me alone for a minute," he grunted, pushing

with all his might against the vines, trying to force his way through.

"Talk to me, Tom."

He was just about ready to say something not so polite, but he held it back as he felt himself begin to move into the opening between the vines.

The pain in his shoulder was sharp, biting, and he hissed through his teeth, turning his head sharply to see what had happened.

"What's the matter, Tom?" the doctor asked. "We're getting some readings here that are starting to concern us."

A thorn was sticking directly into the meat of his arm, easily passing through his skin and into the muscle of his shoulder.

"Dammit," Tom swore, twisting away from the thorn but only managing to cause more pain, this time in his thigh.

He looked down to see that another thorn had pierced him, going through his jeans and into the skin beneath.

Tom's mind raced; he hadn't noticed the thorns there. If he had, he would have been more careful.

"Tom?" the doctor called again, and there was actually concern in his nasally voice.

"The thorns," he managed. "I stuck myself pretty good."

"Get out of there now," Stempler ordered. "Something isn't right."

"Seriously," Tom muttered, taking deep breaths to calm himself. "Give me a minute to . . ."

With growing horror, Tom watched as a thorn grew out from the thick body of a vine close to his chest, the razor-sharp point coming closer and closer still.

He started to scream just before the point of the thorn pierced his flesh. He tried to pull away, but thorns were sprouting all along the bodies of the vines that surrounded him.

"Tom, you have to calm down. Your heart rate has increased to a dangerous level and—"

But Tom wasn't listening anymore, not that he could have answered the doctor even if he'd wanted to. The vines themselves had started to move, squeezing him between their thick mass. He could barely breathe, never mind talk.

More and more thorns erupted from the vines; their spearlike tips seeking out his soft flesh. He could feel himself bleeding from at least six spots, probably more. The wounds had a tendency to grow numb after a time.

The thought crossed Tom's mind again, the question he'd had about whether it was possible to get hurt deep within his subconscious.

It looked like he had his answer.

Tom's body thrashed once on the exam table, then fell limp. A high-pitched warning peal suddenly filled the air, inciting the technicians to action.

"What's happening, Doctor?" Tremain asked, watching as the scientist rose from his seat to check the data output from various machines.

"We've lost him," Stempler said with disbelief. Then, seeing the look on Tremain's face, he quickly added, "He's not dead. But he has fallen so far down into his subconscious that he's apparently unable to communicate with us."

"So he's in a sort of coma?" Tremain offered.

"No, not really," Stempler started to explain when one of the technicians called to him.

"Doctor, come here!"

Tremain and Stempler turned to the table where

Tom lay, the activity around the boy suddenly furious. As they drew closer, alarms sounded and lights flashed.

"What the hell is going on now?" Tremain barked.

Stempler stood frozen, staring at the readouts in disbelief. "I never imagined he'd be able to go so deep," he said.

"You've got two seconds to explain this, Doctor. After that I'm bringing in a med team and—"

"It's really quite amazing," Stempler said, watching as his people adjusted medication flows and repositioned monitors. "The boy—Tom—has entered an altered state of consciousness deep within his mind, in a place of his, or at least his other personality's, creation, where he is now injured. Or so I'm led to believe by his last communication, and his physical body is reacting in kind."

Tremain watched the frantic activity around the boy. "So what exactly are you telling me . . . that if he's hurt or, God forbid, mortally wounded in this dreamland, or wherever the hell he is, he could die?"

The doctor paused for a moment and then nodded. "Yes, it's entirely possible."

Tremain looked back to Tom, at the wires snaking from his body, the spiking lines on the monitors.

"Get him out of there, Doctor," Tremain ordered. "End the experiment—bring him back before it's too late."

Asleep within a dream; how freakin' bizarre is that? Tom thought, suddenly coming awake with the realization that he wasn't anywhere near reality at the moment.

He was lying on a large four-poster bed covered with musty-smelling sheets; the wounds he'd received from the thorny vines had been covered in bandages. The room was dark, the only light from a single burning candle, resting on a dresser top across the room.

Someone had brought him here and seen to his injuries. And he had a sneaking suspicion who it was.

"Bet you thought you was a goner," a low, rasping voice said from a shadowy corner.

Tom sat up quickly, his wounds throbbing, and peered into the darkness. "Tyler?" he asked.

He could barely make out the shape of a chair and a figure slouched there.

"Now, what do you think?" His voice sounded strangely raw. "Got anybody else rattlin' around inside your head? Hope to Christ not; it's already too damn crowded as it is."

Tom squinted into the shadows, trying to see his

alternate self. "You sound different. Is there something wrong with—"

Tyler let out a coarse laugh. "'Is there something wrong?'" he repeated. "That's funny. I like that."

Something in the darkness across from him shifted, and Tom watched as the figure rose from the chair and shambled toward the door. Tyler was wearing what looked to be a blanket, draped over his head and body, hiding his features.

"What's wrong with you?" Tom asked again.

"As if you don't know," Tyler said, passing the bureau, his movement causing the flame of the candle to dance, casting eerie shadows on the walls. "I should have let you die," he continued. "Bled to death on the thorns—but then I'd probably be in worse shape than I am now."

The hunched figure stopped at the door with one hand on the knob. His hand was deathly pale, covered in an angry rash.

"Your hand," Tom said, and watched as Tyler quickly pulled it back, hiding it again beneath the blanket.

"Don't you get it, man?" Tyler said, turning slowly to face him. "You're killing me by inches."

Tom gasped as Tyler removed the blanket—he was looking at his mirror image, only this was a reflection racked with sickness.

"Not a pretty sight, is it?" Tyler asked. His face was deathly pale and gaunt, large open sores on his forehead and cheekbones.

"I don't understand." Tom slid off the bed, the wounds in his legs and arms throbbing painfully as he approached his double.

How was it even possible? Tyler was part of him, and despite the wounds from the thorns, Tom was fine.

"Good sense of humor but dumb as a bag of rocks," Tyler quipped. "What did you think would happen once we started to merge?"

Tom stared, mouth agape.

"Yeah, I knew it. You weren't thinking."

Tyler let the blanket fall from his shoulders. He looked like he'd crawled from the grave: his clothes were in tatters, the exposed flesh teeming with infection.

"Little by little, I'm rotting away."

Tom didn't know what to say. He could only stare in stunned disbelief at his other half, obviously so close to death. He couldn't help but feel sorry for him.

"We were supposed to join," Tom said, interlocking the fingers of both hands. "To merge; how . . . ?"

Tyler shook his head slowly, a scary smiling forming on his sore-covered face. One of the wounds had started to bleed, a scarlet teardrop running down his cheek.

"That's how I thought it would be too," he said, "but then I started to feel what was really happening when I let a little bit of what I am become a part of you—and I didn't care for it." He looked at his hands, as if seeing the decay there for the first time. "I was dying, Tommy," he continued, "and I decided that I didn't want any part of it."

Tom moved closer. "But what choice do you . . . do *we* have?"

The double chuckled. "Jury's still out on which one of us is strongest," he said slyly.

"I told you before." Tom tried to sound tougher than he was actually feeling at the moment, the wounds he'd received from the thorny vines throbbing with the beat of his heart. "I'll never let you take control."

Tyler picked up his blanket from the floor and threw it over his head and shoulders. "You did, didn't you," he said, reaching out and opening the door. "But that puts us smack-dab in the middle of a situation."

Tom followed him into the hallway.

"What do you mean?" he asked, suddenly feeling light-headed, like he just might float away. He leaned back against the bedroom door frame, his vision swimming.

"You're not going anyplace, and neither am I," Tyler said. "But that's something we'll discuss another time."

He turned away and walked toward a pool of darkness at the corridor's end.

"We'll talk about it now!" Tom demanded, pushing off from the door frame and falling to his knees. He didn't know what was wrong, and he wondered if Tyler had done something to weaken him.

"Now why would I do something like that?" Tyler asked, reading his thoughts with a shake of his head. "What do you take me for? If nothing else, I'm fair."

He continued down the hallway toward the patch of darkness. "We'll be seeing each other again," he said casually over his shoulder. "Don't you worry about that."

Tom tried to follow but felt a pull, a serious force intent on extricating him from this environment.

"No." He tried with all his might to fight it, but to no avail. Everything around him went to black as he found himself pulled from the depths of his inner being.

The ascent toward awakening.

It was like coming up from the bottom of a really deep hole.

Tom bolted upright, gasping for air, his heart hammering in his chest, his skin soaked with sweat. It reminded him of the old days, when he'd awaken from a narcoleptic attack, when he'd realize on opening his eyes that the disease had taken him again.

The lab techs swarmed around him, pushing him back, holding him down, tiny flashlight beams shining in his eyes as they bombarded him with questions.

"Do you know what year it is?"

"Can you tell me how old you are?"

"Who is the president of the United States?"

He wanted to answer, but his mouth wouldn't work properly; his attempts at speech came out in a useless garble. It wasn't long before he felt another pinprick of pain in his arm, and the spinning room began to slow, and he was once again embraced by the arms of sleep.

There was no dreaming with this sleep, no doubles with rotting skin, no ancient mansions covered in thorny vines. There was nothing but the deep, dark black and the slowly dawning sense that he was alive.

And then awake.

Tom opened his eyes to see Tremain standing in the corner of the room, cup of steaming coffee in his hand. The man was silent, taking a slow sip from the cup, his eyes unwavering.

"Is something wrong?" Tom slurred, his hands going to his head. He felt like it was wrapped in cotton.

"No," the director replied, moving toward the side

74

of his bed. "Just wanted to be sure you were actually awake this time."

"How long was I out?" Tom asked, the question reminding him of before, when waking up had filled him with a certain amount of trepidation.

"Not long," Tremain said, pulling a chair from beneath a small desk in the corner and sitting at his bedside. "About six hours. They had to pump you full of stuff to make you sleep in order to counteract the stuff they gave to wake you up." He brought his cup up to his mouth. "It's all very complicated. How are you feeling?" he asked, taking a drink.

Tom laid an arm over his eyes. "Honestly? I feel like crap."

"Doesn't surprise me, after everything you've been through."

Planting his hands on either side of the bed, Tom tried to push himself up to a sitting position, only to feel sharp pain throughout his upper body and hammers pounding in his head. He groaned and lay back down.

"What the hell happened to me? I feel like I've been hit by a truck."

"You'd think so, wouldn't you?" Tremain asked. "According to Doc Stempler, when we put you under, you entered an altered state of consciousness so deep that your dream perceptions actually began to manifest on your physical self. Your heart rate skyrocketed and your blood pressure dipped so low they thought they'd lost you for a while. Never mind what your brain waves were doing." He brought the cup of coffee to his mouth again. "Pretty heavy stuff, eh?" he said, before taking another drink.

"This is insane," Tom muttered.

Tremain placed his coffee cup on the floor by his feet. "The doc believes this is all connected to the conditioning Janus used to house two distinct personalities inside your head. He believes the other half is actually an altered perception."

"I don't understand." Tom shook his head, nearly overwhelmed.

"Join the club." Tremain stood. "Being the director of Pandora doesn't necessarily mean that I understand the intricacies of the science behind everything we're involved with. Usually it's not necessary. But now with Kavanagh out there, a threat to all of us . . . I've done my best to get a firm grasp on the logic here, based on what Stempler's explained to me." He paused, and Tom could see that he was trying to think of the best way to explain this latest theory, one that they could both understand.

"Stempler used your eyesight as an example," he

said finally. "Before your two sides started to merge, you needed glasses to improve your vision, but Tyler didn't. His state of being, of having perfect vision, was transferred to you. Your perceptions were altered."

"You're saying my eyes . . . they actually changed—psychically?" Tom knew he didn't need his glasses anymore but hadn't really given it a lot of thought yet. Everything else going on seemed much bigger, but it *was* eerie to suddenly be seeing differently than he had just recently.

"They used to call it mind over matter when I was a kid," Tremain said with a nod.

"So is that why I haven't experienced any narcoleptic attacks?"

"Bingo," Tremain said.

Tom closed his eyes and attempted to process it all. "Who thinks up this stuff anyway, utter maniacs?" he said with a disbelieving laugh.

"No kidding," the director said, reaching down to pick up the empty cup from the floor.

He returned the chair to the desk and looked back at Tom. "The human animal is a fascinating creature, Tom. Full of great intelligence and imagination—always reaching to understand more about the ways things work and how to make things better, but we're also kind of twisted."

"And that's where something like me comes from," Tom said.

Tremain nodded. "And why the Pandora Group exists." He started toward the door. "If you only knew the kinds of things that have been created by supposedly civilized minds, you'd never leave that bed."

"Minds like Brandon Kavanagh's," Tom said, watching as the director stopped at the door.

"Just like Brandon Kavanagh's," he agreed. "And he used to be one of the good guys, if you can imagine that."

"You're afraid of him, aren't you?" Tom asked.

"I'm afraid of the threat he poses, yes," Tremain said. "The sooner we have him in custody—"

"Or dead," Tom interjected.

Tremain seemed to think about that. "Or dead," he concurred. "The better off we'll all be."

Tom closed his eyes again, feeling himself grow more tired by the second. "Give me a chance to rest up, and we can try to reach Tyler again. Something tells me there are all kinds of secrets locked away inside my head and . . ."

"We just have to figure a way to get them out," Tremain finished, the last words Tom heard before falling fast asleep.

CHAPTER 6

Tom sat at the edge of his hospital bed, waiting for his escort.

That was probably the thing that irked him most about being at the Pandora facility: he was never allowed to go anywhere unescorted, which made it seem like they didn't trust him. And to be perfectly honest, after what he'd experienced the last few days, he didn't really blame them.

The disturbing image of a gaunt and sickly Tyler Garrett filled his mind. It was horrifying to know something like that was inside him. A knock at the door interrupted his thoughts, and he slipped on his sneakers before answering.

Agent Catherine Mayer waited in the hallway. "You call for an escort?" she asked, smiling.

He liked Mayer; she was the agent he saw most

often, but best of all, she didn't treat him like some kind of science project reject.

And there was something about her, maybe the shape her mouth took when she smiled, that reminded him of his mother. *No, not my mother.* He had to keep reminding himself that the woman he'd known as Victoria Lovett was no relation to him at all.

He felt a stab of pain and silently cursed himself as he checked the hospital room to make sure he wasn't leaving anything behind. It wouldn't do him any good to dwell on the past. He had to concentrate on the future.

"Ready?" Mayer asked, and Tom nodded as he joined her in the hall.

The two waved at the nurse behind the desk on their way to the elevators up to Tom's living quarters.

"Are you feeling better?" Mayer asked as the elevator doors closed.

"Yeah, thanks," he answered, smiling. It was amazing how such a small gesture could go so far toward making him feel human again.

The elevator came to a stop, and Tom was ready to step out when the doors opened to admit Tremain and Agent Abernathy. Tom could see a hint of bruising around Abnernathy's jaw and eye, a painful reminder of their fight earlier in the week. The man gave him a look that could freeze blood.

Both men were armed and wearing bulletproof vests. Tom knew that Abernathy was in charge of field operations, and his curiosity was immediately piqued.

Mayer gently placed a hand on Tom's chest, pushing him back farther into the elevator to allow the two men to enter.

"Sir," she said, acknowledging Tremain.

The director gave her a nod, briefly making eye contact with Tom before turning away to continue his conversation with Abernathy.

There was something in that look, something that triggered some kind of instinct in Tom—a sixth sense connected to his other half. Whatever was happening had something to do with him.

He concentrated on their whispers, thinking he heard mention of Chicago, which only served to make him more jittery.

The elevator stopped again, and as the doors parted, Tremain and Abernathy stepped off. Tom could hear the murmuring of activity on the floor, and suddenly he darted around Agent Mayer. She cried out and lunged for him, but he was faster and slid through the narrow opening just as the elevator doors closed. He felt bad about ditching his escort, but something was up, and he was sure he should be a part of it.

He had stepped into a large conference room. A

huge map of Illinois hung on the wall in front of a meeting table. Satellite photos of various neighborhoods were clipped to the edges of the map.

A rock formed in the pit of his stomach as suspicion started to take shape.

Abernathy was the first to notice that Tom was behind them. "Hey, you don't belong here," he snarled, moving toward him, and Tom immediately assumed a fighting stance, ready to take on the agent again.

"Stand down, Agent," Tremain said wearily as he stepped toward them. "You can't be here, Tom."

"I overheard you talking," he said. "You're going to Chicago—does this have anything to do with Madison?"

He carefully watched the director's face, looking for the slightest hint that he was right, and he caught it—a telltale twitch at the corner of the man's right eye.

"What's going on?" he demanded.

The elevator doors opened and an exasperated Agent Mayer stormed out. "I'm sorry, sir, he was just too fast for me. . . ."

"Is she in danger, Mr. Tremain?" Tom asked over the harried agent. "You have to tell me."

"We don't have to tell you anything," Abernathy blurted, reaching to take hold of his arm. "You're to return to your quarters with Agent Mayer at once and—"

Without even thinking, Tom grabbed hold of Abernathy's hand and bent the fingers back. The agent screamed out in pain and dropped to his knees.

"Let him go, Tom," Tremain ordered, and Tom did.

Abernathy scowled, and Tom was certain that if Tremain hadn't been there, things would have gotten very ugly. But instead, the agent composed himself, stepping back, allowing his boss to handle the situation.

"We've received intelligence that Kavanagh is moving against a target in a Chicago suburb and—"

"It's Madison," Tom interrupted. "Her mother lives in the Chicago suburbs, and if Kavanagh is sending somebody to hurt her, we have to do something immediately."

Tremain put his arm around his shoulders and steered him toward the elevator. "We have a team working on it right now. Go back to your room and we'll keep you posted."

"Let me go with you," Tom said, planting his feet and shrugging off the director's comforting arm.

"You know that's impossible, Tom," Tremain replied. "It's a trap. Kavanagh is using Madison to get to us, to you. This is our chance to turn the tables on him. We'll contact you just as soon as we hear anything."

"You know I have the skills," Tom said desperately.

"And you know that the more I use them, the better I get. And who knows what I could remember while I'm out in the field—things we're all trying to learn here at the lab, which doesn't seem all that much safer anyway."

Abernathy came forward as Tremain remained silent.

"You can't be serious, sir," he said. "You're aware of the risks—"

"I'm very aware, Agent Abernathy," Tremain snapped.

The director's gaze had gone icy cold, and Tom had to wonder what exactly Tremain was seeing as he looked at him.

Kenny Tibideau was getting one of *those* headaches, the kind that usually led to trouble of one kind or another. Sometimes he heard voices when his head ached. He wasn't sure exactly what it meant, maybe he was crazy, but it was a problem he'd had for just about as long as he could remember—a problem that was his and his alone.

He ignored the pain and squinted through the driver's side window, concentrating on the house numbers as he slowly drove by.

He'd always suspected that hearing voices would be the one last thing his parents would need to put him away for good. That, on top of the fact that he'd been born with a rare sleep disorder.

Nope, the whispering voice that he heard from time to time would always be his little secret. And besides, it didn't do any real harm, reminding him a lot of a radio signal not quite tuned in. It was more annoying than anything else, especially because it sometimes led to one of his narcoleptic attacks.

If he was going to have one, he hoped he could hold it off at least until he delivered the pizza.

Kenny glanced at his watch and felt a stab of panic. He had less then six minutes to make his delivery or the customer paid nothing. He glanced over to the red thermal bag resting on the seat beside him; so much pressure for one large pepperoni, one super-Caesar salad, and one order of cheesy bread sticks.

He really didn't know why he stayed with the job; it didn't pay all that great, and the tips often weren't worth the trouble of finding a house on a late Friday night in the wilds of the Chicago suburbs. His boss, Mr. K., could be a real ballbuster, but at the same time he was an all-right guy. A full physical was required to work for Mama Mia Pizza, and of course his problem— his narcolepsy—had come up, but Mr. K. didn't seem to care. *As long as you do the job, we won't have a problem,* he'd said.

Finding the house at last, Kenny pulled the delivery car over to the curb. *Just in time*, was his last thought before everything went black.

Slumping momentarily in the seat, the boy soon recovered. He sat up and looked around with new eyes.

Kenny Tibideau wasn't there anymore. He'd been replaced by another who wore his skin, one with an entirely different objective.

A portable phone trilled inside the glove compartment, and the boy reached across to retrieve it.

"Is everything set, Sleeper Two?" a voice asked him.

The boy peeled back the Velcro cover to expose the carrier's contents: the large pizza box and paper bag containing the salad and the bread sticks. He lifted the lid of the pizza box to expose not a large pepperoni, but a twelve-shot Beretta compact pistol.

"Are you prepared for delivery?" the voice asked again as he closed the box lid.

"Affirmative," the boy said before switching off the phone and returning it to the glove compartment.

Then he got out of the car, food case balanced on one arm, and strolled up the walkway toward the house.

To make his delivery.

Madison tapped her foot uneasily. They were all sitting together in the living room, she and her mother at opposite ends of the couch and her father across from them in the old wing-backed chair. No one would make eye contact.

"I can't stand this," Madison finally blurted. "Why do you two have to act so childish?"

"Honey," her mother said, staring at her manicured nails. "It's been a long night for all of us. Let's not get start—"

"Mom," Madison interrupted, jumping up from the couch. "Don't tell me not to get started. Ever since I got home all you two have done is fight, and now you won't even speak to each other."

"Madison, please," her mother begged. "I'm tired."

"I know," Madison said. "I know you're tired, and so am I. Do you even have any idea what I've been through the past couple of weeks?" She stopped, cutting herself off as she realized how close she'd been to spilling the fact that she'd completely fallen for an amazing guy who just happened to be a sleeper assassin, which he hadn't even discovered himself until just after she met him.

She couldn't tell her parents the truth about Tom. She couldn't tell anyone.

But God, didn't they get that there was bigger stuff out there than stupid fights about the mortgage or whatever?

"I just . . . I just wish you could remember that we all used to be a family," Madison continued, lowering her voice. "And okay, you aren't together anymore, and I get that that's not going to change. But could you at least be civil to each other, for my sake? And yours?"

"We know it's been hard for you," her mom said. She shot a look over at Madison's father, then went on. "Your father and I had spoken about how to handle this before you came back, and I *thought* we were on the same page about making this as easy as possible on you."

"Maybe it would be best if I headed out," her father said, an edge to his voice. He stood, a deep frown creasing his forehead.

"No, we need to talk about this," Madison said, surprising herself with how firm and reasonable she sounded. It was weird, but now that she was home, it was really hitting her how much everything she'd just experienced had changed her. How could she be afraid to confront her parents and try to force them to be adults about their problems after facing off against trained killers? "With everything that's happened," she finished, "I can't believe you two are being so selfish."

"We're not being selfish," her father replied sternly. "We've been trying to do what's best for you."

"You—" Madison began, but was interrupted by the sound of the doorbell.

"Who the hell could that be?" her mother muttered, looking at the time.

"I'll get it," her dad said, striding to the door.

For a moment Madison and her mother sat and listened to the sound of her father's voice wafting in from the foyer.

"Who is he talking to?" her mother asked, pushing off from the couch. Madison got up to follow.

"Hey, guys?" he called out then. "We didn't order a pizza, did we?"

CHAPTER

7

Tom was amazed at how quickly everything was moving.

As he sat in the back of the van speeding through the nighttime streets of Chicago, his thoughts were a blur, and he made a conscious effort to slow them.

He had been shocked when Tremain actually seemed to believe that there was merit in his suggestion and had invited him into the debriefing, much to the displeasure of Agent Abernathy.

In the darkness of the van Tom glanced casually in the agent's direction. He was sitting with his eyes closed at the end of a row of three other blank-faced Pandora agents. *Mentally preparing for the mission ahead,* Tom thought, *or maybe just catching up on some sleep.*

It had been nonstop activity since leaving Washington. A caravan of vans had left Pandora for a short ride to a private airfield where a jet had been waiting for them. The team had been airborne almost immediately. An hour and thirty-seven minutes later they had landed just outside Chicago and hooked up with another, smaller group of agents. It had been a whirlwind, but at least they'd been on the move toward Madison.

Tom rubbed his hands together nervously, wishing that the van would move faster.

"Are they sweating?" Tremain asked from his seat beside him.

Tom turned to look at him. "Excuse me?"

"I asked if they were sweating," he said, motioning with his chin. "Your hands—are your hands sweaty?"

"A little," Tom said.

"Been in this business an awfully long time and my hands still get that way," he said.

Tom could see the agents around them responding to the director's words: small knowing smiles and nodding heads, some agents even looking at their own hands and then rubbing them on their pant legs.

"Besides the sweaty hands," he said, "are you doing all right? If not, it's perfectly okay for you to stay with the van and—"

"No," Tom interrupted. "I'm fine; it's just that I'm worried . . . about her."

Tremain was quiet, which did nothing to lessen his concern.

"Why her?" Tom asked. "Why are they after Madison? What does she have to do with anything?"

Tremain leaned his head back against wall of the van. "Kavanagh is a really sore loser. Something of great value has been taken from him, and now he's going to strike back."

Tom stared, not sure if he really understood.

"You, Tom," the director continued. "You're the thing that's been taken away."

"But it still doesn't explain why Madison." Tom was desperate for an answer that would make some sort of sense to him.

"I'm sure that Kavanagh is well aware of how fond of the girl you've become," Tremain said coldly. "He's using her to pull you in. She and anyone unlucky enough to be with her at the time are going to be made examples."

Tom still couldn't believe it. "So he's gonna try and kill her because he's pissed off at me? That's insane."

The director nodded. "That's Brandon Kavanagh. This is his way of flipping off Pandora—to show that he isn't afraid, a warning not to mess with his plans."

Tom felt his anger surge, his thoughts going to the eerie dream image of his other self—Tyler Garrett, fleeing deeper into the old mansion, deeper into the recesses of his mind.

Where the secrets were kept.

"But we *are* going to mess with him, right?" he asked the director.

"Oh yes," Tremain answered with a serious nod. "You can count on that."

"Good," Tom said, pulling back on his anger. "And when we get back to Pandora, I want to let Dr. Stempler have another try at me."

"That isn't necessary, Tom," Tremain said. "I'm sure there are other, less dangerous methods we could use to—"

"There isn't enough time," Tom interrupted. "He has to be stopped. Look what Kavanagh's done to me . . . what he's trying to do to Madison and her family."

He turned his gaze to the director, looking into the older man's eyes. "Who's next?" he asked.

"Sorry, pal," Madison heard her father say as she entered the hall behind her mother. "Think you've got the wrong house."

She glanced toward the foyer, where her mother had joined her father. "What address do you have?" her mother asked.

From where she stood, Madison could see the kid

fumbling with a large pizza box and a delivery bag. *Probably his first run or something,* she thought as she heard him muttering under his breath.

Madison laughed quietly, shaking her head. "Dude, it's not the house," she said softly to herself. It seemed like the beginning of a bad joke—*How long does it take a pizza guy to realize he's gone to the wrong house?*

The sudden sound made her jump, as if somebody had set off a firecracker. She looked up to see her father stumbling backward, bent over, hands clutched to his stomach.

"Daddy?" she asked, watching in slow motion as he turned around. There was blood on his hands—on the front of his shirt. He looked almost as surprised as she was.

Her mother was trying to keep him from falling. She was screaming his name over and over again, and Madison finally realized that her father had been shot.

The deliveryman—no, he was just a kid, like her— moved into the house, smoking pistol in hand, and shot her mother.

Ohmygod, ohmygod, ohmygod, ohmygod, ohmygod, ohmygod.

Madison screamed as the next shot rang out and her mother fell to the floor, dragging her father down with her.

And then the gunman looked at Madison, and she saw something in his eyes, something cold, inhuman, and horribly familiar.

Her mind was deluged with memories of the last few weeks. And looking at this guy, who now aimed the barrel of a gun at her, she realized that the violence had managed to follow her—tracking her to her very door.

Her parents were moving—both alive for now, but for how much longer Madison hadn't a clue. She watched as the deliveryman aimed, his finger nearing the trigger, and then she reacted. It wasn't the smartest thing to do, but her resources were limited.

She screamed as loudly as she could, then grabbed at the first thing she saw—a sneaker from the floor—and threw it at the attacker. The shoe hit him square in the face, and he flinched. He was already moving toward her, once again aiming his pistol. Still, she ran, practically feeling the gun on the back of her head.

Then she heard a commotion behind her and spun around to see that her father had risen from the floor and grabbed hold of the gunman's arm. The gun went off, but the shot was wild, shattering a table lamp nearby.

"Get away," her father was screaming, and she saw blood dripping from the corner of his mouth and down his neck.

She hesitated a moment but then understood the look in his eyes. He was going to sacrifice everything for her.

He's going to die if he has to, she thought as she turned and ran through the house.

The caravan turned onto Washington Street and pulled over to the curb, not far from the Fitzgeralds' home.

"This is it, people," Tremain said, and a kind of electric buzz went through the back of the vehicle as each of the agents readied to perform the function assigned him or her.

He turned to Tom and, in a fatherly gesture, reached over adjust the straps of the boy's bulletproof vest. "You sure about this?"

"I'm good," Tom replied, his body tingling in anticipation. "So what now?"

"We wait," Tremain said coolly.

"You're kidding," Tom said incredulously, rising from his seat. He felt the other agents' eyes on him. "We're just going to sit here? What if they're in danger or . . . ?"

Tremain gestured for him to sit. "Easy, Tom," he said. "We've had the place under surveillance since we learned of the threat."

Abernathy cleared his throat, and they all looked to the front of the van, where the agent was pulling off a headset and frowning. "We've lost contact with the surveillance team, sir. Could be a—"

Tom didn't wait for the man to finish. He lunged for the van exit, sliding the door across and leaping from the vehicle onto the street. Instincts becoming increasingly familiar to him had kicked in, instincts that told him time was of the essence.

His eyes scanned the street for the obvious federal vehicle that the surveillance team would be using, and he decided on a dark, fairly new Chrysler parked on the opposite side of the street. A quick glance into the car showed two operatives, both dead from shots to the head at close range.

Tom ran down the street, spotting a car with a Mama Mia Pizza logo parked not too far away. He felt a sickening pit open up in his stomach and raced toward the house, knowing full well that a delivery was one of the easiest ways to hit a house. He was thinking like a killer, and if he hadn't been so concerned for Madison's safety, he probably would have gotten sick right there on the street.

He approached the front door and found it ajar. Saying a silent prayer that he wasn't too late, he placed his fingertips on the door, slowly pushing it open. He was greeted by the grisly sight of a man, his front spattered with gore, leaning against the wall, a woman lying with her head in his lap.

Tom's eyes darted around the foyer as he slowly entered the house, heading toward the couple. He noticed a blood-spattered pizza box lying discarded on the floor but thankfully, no sign of Madison.

Her parents looked pretty bad, though. He reached out a hand toward the man to check for a pulse and was startled when he began to cough. The woman remained still, and he laid his fingertips on her wrist. Her pulse was weak, but at least there was one.

They were alive, for now.

He thought about going back outside, meeting the Pandora agents that were sure to be following, but one thought kept him right where he was.

Where's Madison?

He had to find her. His senses were alive, eyes scanning the living room and adjacent dining room, ears alert. There were two bullet holes in the living room wall and one in the dining room. *There was a pursuit*, he thought, moving quickly from one room to an area that would either take him into the kitchen to the left or up a stairway. He noticed another bullet hole in the wall going upstairs. Madison must have headed up there.

Tom was amazed at his sense of calm. He felt himself

just going along for the ride, allowing the instincts that he had inherited from his opposite persona to flow freely.

The last step before reaching the landing at the top of the stairs creaked loudly, and he pulled his foot away, listening for any sign that his presence was known.

Hearing nothing, he crept onto the landing. At the end of the hallway was a room, its door partially open, a light glowing from within, and he carefully, stealthily moved toward it.

There was an explosion of movement to his left as someone emerged from a linen closet near him, and he caught sight of an aluminum baseball bat careening toward his head. Tom reacted in an instant, one hand reaching up to capture the bat, halting its swing, the other coming around to make a thrust into his attacker's throat, collapsing the fragile trachea.

And then he froze, seeing the face of his attacker. "Madison," he said, his hand turning from lethal weapon to just a hand and reaching out to cup her frightened face.

Her expression changed from sheer terror to absolute relief, and she fell into his arms. "I can't believe you're here," she said into his chest, and for the briefest of moments, as he held her like that, everything seemed okay.

Madison suddenly tensed in his arms and screamed, "Tom, watch out!"

And he reacted immediately, spinning around, pushing her out of the way so that he was between her and the explosion of gunfire.

The bullet entered the meat of his shoulder and he grunted with pain, but already he was isolating the agony, storing it away where it wouldn't hinder his actions.

The gunman was ready to fire again, and Tom ran toward him, dropping to the floor and rolling beneath the shot. He sprang to his feet, swatting the pistol from the guy's hand.

The attacker reacted in an instant, launching a roundhouse kick that connected with the side of Tom's face. He dropped to his knees, trying to clear the ringing and sudden vertigo that made his head swim, but the attacker was already on the move, retrieving the pistol from the floor and making ready to put a bullet into Tom's skull.

Tom had tensed to spring when a voice called out.

"Stay where you are!" it screamed, and a series of five shots followed. The first was a head shot, the other four direct hits to the chest and heart. The young man stumbled and fell backward, dead before he hit the floor.

Tom knew that voice and reacted instinctively, diving for the Beretta dropped by his attacker, snatching it up from the ground and spinning around to take aim.

"Hello, Tom," his mother said. She was standing at the top of the stairs, still squinting down the barrel of the smoldering gun. "I didn't expect to see you here."

The killer instinct told Tom to fire, to send a bullet into the face of the woman who had so devastatingly betrayed him.

Madison stood frozen by the hallway closet, her eyes flicking between him and his mother. Tom was certain she was wondering the same thing he was.

Can I do it?

His finger stroked the metal trigger of the Beretta as he aimed down the barrel, past the sight.

"What are you doing here, Tom?" The woman lowered her own weapon.

He wanted to shoot her, to make her pay—make her hurt for all the pain that she had caused him. But he couldn't do it. No matter how loudly part of him screamed for him to fire the weapon, there was another part of him, an even stronger instinct, that recognized the woman as his mother. A mother he'd believed was already dead until this moment.

He dropped the gun, and it fell to the hallway floor with a loud clatter. The woman began to move toward him, but Madison stepped around him and blocked her path.

"Tom, there's something—" his mother started to say, but the hallway was suddenly filled with the screams and yells of Pandora agents.

Like angry bees they swarmed up the stairs, their weapons drawn, hollering for everyone to hit the deck. Tom dropped to his knees, eyes on his mother as the agents bore down on her with their weapons aimed.

Maybe one of them will have the courage, he thought, struggling with rabid emotions flowing through him. He despised her and loved her. She was the last living thing from a life he believed dead, and in her eyes he saw it all. And he wanted it back.

"Are you all right, Tom?" Tremain asked, taking his arm and pulling him to his feet.

Tom watched them drag her down the hallway toward the stairs. She was straining to see him over her shoulder. "What do *you* think?" he said to Tremain, yanking his arm away. He felt the sudden scream of pain from the bullet wound in his shoulder, but next to everything else, it barely even registered.

•   •   •

The electric buzzer on the door sounded shrilly as its lock disengaged, allowing Tremain access to the interrogation room where the woman, whose last known identity was Victoria Lovett, was being detained.

He was holding two plastic foam cups of coffee and placed one down in front of her, along with two creamers and three packets of sugar.

"Haven't a clue how you like it," he said, pulling out a chair and sitting across from her at the plain metal table. He had a file folder under his arm and set it down on the table in front of him.

"Thank you," she responded politely, pulling the cup of coffee closer.

The director of operations opened the file and slowly perused its contents.

"Is that on me?" the woman asked as she tore open two sugar packets and poured their contents into the hot fluid.

"Mmmm," he grunted as he continued to read.

"Can't imagine it's all that interesting." She picked up one of the creamers.

"On the contrary, Ms. . . . ." Tremain paused and looked up from the open file. "Would you like me to use your real name, or would you prefer one of your ten aliases?" He smiled kindly, watching as she finished pouring another creamer into her coffee.

"Victoria will be fine," she replied. "I've become comfortable with the name." She lifted the coffee to her lips and took a careful sip. "I've grown quite fond of it, actually."

"Then Victoria it is," he said good-naturedly, turning over a few of the documents within the folder.

The woman was a spy, and a good one at that. She had begun her career in military intelligence, eventually leaving the service of her country and losing herself in the freelance world of espionage.

"Let me start by saying how surprised we are to see you alive." Tremain looked intensely across the table at her. "We thought you had been killed in the explosions," he said, referring to the recent events in Hawthorne, Massachusetts.

Victoria shook her head, placing the cup of coffee back on the table. "I made it out through the sliding door in the back of the Arsenaults' house," she explained casually. "I got cut up pretty good with some flying glass." She lifted the sleeve of her shirt to show off various healing cuts and abrasions. "But other than that, I'm fine."

"And your husband?"

"He wasn't my husband," she quickly corrected.

Tremain smiled coldly. "All right, then, did your . . . partner survive?"

"No," she replied. "He wasn't as lucky as I was."

She's a cool one; I'll give her that, Tremain thought, observing her reactions as they spoke. It was as if they were talking about something as casual as the weather.

He flipped past a few more documents, interested to see if he could ruffle some feathers. She had worked for both sides, drifting to whoever would pay her the most. She didn't appear to have any loyalties, which made this situation even more surprising, for here she sat, apparently still working for Brandon Kavanagh.

"Do you know this young man?" Tremain asked, removing a crime scene photo taken at the Fitzgerald house and sliding it to the center of the table. It was a shot of the teenage deliveryman lying dead on the hallway floor.

Victoria leaned forward for a better look. "I was his handler on this particular assignment," she answered.

"But from what I understand," Tremain continued, "you're the one who killed him."

She took another careful sip of her coffee. "That's right."

"Why?"

"He was going to hurt my son."

The director stared at her for a moment. "Tom is not your son," he said, and for the first time he could see that his words had an effect.

She glared at him with a coldness that hinted at

what she could be capable of if given the opportunity.

"But he is," she said, holding the base of her coffee cup and slowly turning it around. "For a while he was my son—and I actually started to believe it." Victoria looked up, staring directly into Tremain's eyes. "Isn't that the craziest thing you've ever heard?" she asked him incredulously. "You're looking at my file. Can you believe it? Because I certainly can't."

She fell silent, and Tremain tried to decide if he was witnessing an actual emotional response or simply an Academy Award–winning performance.

"You were this boy's handler," he said, removing a picture of Tom from the file and sliding it across the table to her.

"Yes," she whispered, staring at the photo.

"The young man you shot tonight—were he and Tom alike in any way?"

Victoria looked up from the photo. "Were they both sleeper operatives—products of the Janus Project? Yes, yes, they were. Is that what you want to hear, Mr. Tremain?"

"Then you're still working for Brandon Kavanagh," the director stated bluntly.

"As of a few hours ago, yes, but now . . . I'm not quite so sure," she answered with a nervous shake of her head.

"Where is he?" Tremain asked.

She was staring at him again, her eyes boring into his. "Why was Tom with you tonight?" She countered with her own question.

"Where is Brandon Kavanagh?" Tremain repeated, ignoring her question.

"Answer me first," Victoria demanded. "Why was Tom there?"

Tremain stared at her for a moment. "I believed he would be an asset to the mission," he said flatly. "Now, you tell me, where is Kavanagh?"

"I want to speak with Tom."

"Do you know the whereabouts of Brandon Kavanagh?" Tremain repeated the words slowly, his voice rising, loud in the confines of the tiny room.

"I need to speak with my son."

He slammed his hands down on the tabletop, causing the nearly empty plastic coffee cups to dance. "Tell me where he is!" he shouted.

Victoria matched his steely stare, unaffected by his loss of composure. "Let me speak with my son and I'll tell you everything I know."

Tremain stood, gathering his papers and photos and placing them back inside the folder. His mind raced. This could be the opportunity he'd been waiting for, but it would again require the boy to be involved, and could he really trust this woman?

Silently he walked to the door, rapping three times as a signal to the guards on the other side.

He would need to give this deal some serious consideration.

The door unlocked with an irritating buzz, and he was just about to step out of the interrogation room when she called to him.

"Mr. Tremain?"

He turned to look at her. She appeared perfectly calm—in control.

"Thank you for the coffee," she said.

"Thank you," Tom said to Agent Mayer as they walked down the hallway toward the room that Madison Fitzgerald had vacated just a few short days ago.

Agent Mayer looked conflicted, and Tom felt a momentary pang of regret. He did like her; she was the only one who seemed human, not just a Pandora drone. He hated knowing that helping him out like this would probably land her in major trouble. But they had kept him away from Madison since they'd come back from Chicago, and he was desperate to see her.

Another agent was posted outside Madison's room, and Mayer approached her. The two women began an animated conversation, and Tom could tell that the other agent wasn't thrilled about disobeying orders either, but Mayer exerted her authority and the woman buckled.

Mayer looked in Tom's direction, gesturing for him to approach. The other agent refused to look at him.

"Let's make this quick," Mayer told him as he knocked on the door.

He agreed with a nod, again thanking her with his eyes.

"Madison, it's me," he called out, and heard the sound of hurried movement from within.

The door was pulled open, and Madison stood there. Tom was shocked by her appearance. She was pale, her eyes swollen and red, her cheeks blotchy with tears. She took his hand and pulled him inside the room, closing the door, then throwing her trembling body into his. He didn't know what to say, but clearly words weren't what she needed anyway. He tentatively put his arms around her, holding her, allowing her to cry, saying nothing. It felt good, being there for her. He would give her as much of his strength as she wanted. It was the least he could do for her.

Gradually Madison stopped trembling and finally pulled away from him, her face damp with tears. "I don't even know if they're alive," she said, her voice sounding on the verge of tears again.

"They are," he said quickly, and went on to tell her

the information that Agent Mayer had shared with him earlier. Madison's parents had been brought to the Pandora medical facility. It had been touch-and-go for a while, especially for Madison's mother, but even though both were still in critical condition, they were now stable.

Madison's hands went to her face, wiping the tears away, her strength returning as a glimmer of hope appeared. "So they're going to be all right?" she asked.

Tom nodded, watching as the information began to sink in.

Madison's whole expression relaxed, her eyes the brightest green Tom had ever seen.

"Thank you, thank you," she repeated over and over. She grabbed him again and held him tight, kissing his neck and the side of his face.

Then she pulled back slightly, meeting his gaze. Her lips were just inches from his, and Tom looked down at her, wanting nothing more than to finally show her how much she meant to him. And suddenly their lips met, and she was kissing him, a full-on kiss. All Tom could think about was her in his arms, their lips pressed together. It was everything he'd imagined—except better.

Madison was the first to break away. She smiled at him, her expression seeming to communicate something so much deeper than gratitude as she stroked the back of his head. He bent to kiss her again.

"Thank you," she whispered softly against his neck. "Thank you for coming to my rescue—for being here."

A lead weight suddenly dropped into the pit of Tom's stomach. None of this would even have happened to her if it wasn't for him. He pulled away from her.

"What is it?" she asked him. "I don't want to sound needy; I just really appreciate what you've done and—"

He shook his head. "No, no, it's not that."

"Tom, what's wrong?" she asked again.

"It's me," he said, feeling his anger build. "This is all about me."

"I don't understand. . . ."

"If it wasn't for me, everything in your life would be fine. Your parents would be fine—your aunt and uncle would be fine. For Christ's sake, their house would still be standing." He backed up, completely ashamed. "Your life wouldn't be in danger. It's all because of me."

He felt like a yawning void had suddenly formed between them—a powerful blackness pushing them apart.

"Tom, I—" Madison began, but she never got the opportunity to finish.

Without even a knock, the door to her room opened, and Christian Tremain strode inside. Tom could see the two agents in the hallway behind the director, both looking like they had just been read the riot act.

"Sir, I—"

Tremain raised a hand, and Tom fell silent. The look on the man's face told him that things other than his own unauthorized visit to Madison were on his mind.

"It's your mother, Tom," he started.

"She's not my—" Tom interrupted, feeling a spark of anger.

"She wants to speak to you," Tremain continued firmly. "And for the good of everyone involved, I suggest you do so."

Brandon Kavanagh loved to visit the implantation chamber.

He stood in the quiet semidarkness, captivated by the sight of the young bodies lying restrained on the hospital beds, their shaved heads adorned with multiple colored wires and cables feeding information directly into their brains.

Kavanagh glanced at his watch, making note of the time. He was curious as to how his plans outside the facility were progressing.

The door into the chamber opened, and a lab tech, his face buried in some file data, entered the room. "Oh, excuse me, sir," he said with a start. "I didn't realize you were in here."

"Quite all right," Kavanagh replied, looking back to the beds. "How are they doing?"

The tech approached a control station and set down his clipboard. "As far as we can tell, they're doing fine," he answered. "Data absorption is occurring in all eight—"

"Seven," Kavanagh corrected, pointing to the empty bed at the end.

The tech chuckled. "Right, seven," he replied with a shake of his head. "I keep forgetting one of the new batch is in use. Anyway, data absorption is moving along quite nicely." He leaned in to look at one of the computer monitors at his station. "It looks like we're up to firearm use right now," the tech said, glancing up with a grin. "It's all smooth sailing, as far as I can see."

If only I could believe that, Kavanagh mused, just as the door to the implantation chamber opened again and Noah Wells strode in. "A word with you, sir?" Wells said, clearing his throat.

Kavanagh glanced at the lab tech, his message passing to the man without him saying a word.

"If you'll excuse me," the tech said quickly, giving Wells a wide berth as he went out the door.

"What have I ever done to him?" Wells asked, irritated.

"Perhaps you give off a bad vibe," Kavanagh suggested.

"Do you think?" he asked. "I guess it would explain a lot."

Kavanagh was again studying the occupants of the

beds. "So, what do you have for me?" he asked. "Was Sleeper Two successful?" He reached out a hand, grabbing hold of the cold metal of a bed's railing.

"I'm afraid not, sir," Wells answered. "Sleeper Two was killed at the scene before he could complete his assignment."

"Pandora?" Kavanagh asked, already knowing the likely answer but wanting to be sure.

"Yes. Tremain was there, as well as the boy."

He looked away from the beds. "Tyler was there?"

Wells nodded. "We believe it was him, yes."

Kavanagh was silent, absorbing the information as he listened to the sounds of the machines that kept the sleepers locked in slumber.

"And the woman—Sleeper Two's handler . . ." Wells began.

Kavanagh could hear the tension in the man's voice. "Go on," he urged.

"Pandora took her into custody."

Kavanagh closed his eyes and breathed a sigh of relief.

"Are you all right, sir?" Wells asked.

"I'm fine, Noah," he answered, turning back to the beds. He had decided he would spend a little more time with the products of his genius.

"It's all smooth sailing, as far as I can see."

He wished that it could be done another way—*any* other way.

Tom had never felt so conflicted—absolute joy, overwhelming sadness, a burning anger, all tore through him in a matter of seconds—all because of her.

He stood just inside the doorway of the tiny interrogation room, the sound of the door locking behind him repeating over and over in his head. A sound that told him there was no turning back.

Concentrating on the scuffed linoleum floor, he refused to look at the woman before him.

Tremain had brought him directly here from Madison's room, explaining how vital it was that Tom get the prisoner to talk. He'd tried to explain that he would rather endure Dr. Stempler's tests 24/7 than spend five minutes with this woman. Tom was desperate for there to be another way, but then Tremain had said that she knew where Kavanagh was, and he'd felt that familiar anger beginning to rise. Tom knew that he'd do just about anything to find the man who had destroyed his life.

"I'll bet I'm the last person you want to see right now," a painfully familiar voice said, distracting him from his thoughts.

Tom started to look up from the floor but stopped himself. There actually was a part of him that wanted to see her again, that same part that wanted so desperately to be taken in her arms and told that this was all bad dream, that when he woke up, everything would be fine.

But that part of him was as dumb as a bag of rocks, because all of that stuff about feeling safe in her arms was a lie. *She* was nothing but a lie.

He wanted to say something smart—something really insulting to show that she wasn't anything to him anymore—but he couldn't think of a thing. For the briefest of moments he wished that Tyler were in control. He'd know exactly what to say.

"However you're feeling—about me, I'm really glad you've come."

He must've looked like a complete idiot, standing by the door, fists clenched, staring at the ground.

"Do you want to sit down?"

Tom lurched toward the table, his gaze moving up from the floor to the back of the metal chair—but not to her. He sat down and immediately felt his panic begin to rise. He half expected his off-the-wall emotional state to trigger a narcoleptic attack, but it didn't. He hadn't experienced an attack since the first steps in merging with his alternate personality.

It was actually sort of exciting, the only really good thing to come out of the whole nasty Janus business, although a good narcoleptic attack would have been the perfect way to remove himself from this painful situation.

"Would you like some water?" she asked, and Tom heard her removing the cellophane wrapping from a plastic cup.

Tom said nothing. He didn't want water from her— he wanted nothing, other than to get the hell out of there.

"Tom, look at me," she ordered with a stab of parental authority, and instinctually he did as he was told.

She was staring at him as she poured water from a plastic pitcher into the unwrapped cup. "I know this is hard for you," she said, sliding the cup over to him. "But we have to talk."

He took the cup in his hand, careful not to crush it in his angry grip. "I have nothing to say to you," he said, averting his eyes again.

"But I have things to say to you," she said as she poured some water for herself. "Important things that can't wait any longer."

He stood and moved back toward the door. "I can't sit here and listen to any more of your lies."

"Please, Tom," she begged, and all he heard was the woman who had loved and cared for him. "Not everything was a lie."

He found himself pulled to her voice and turned to see that she was standing too, holding her arms out to him.

"I really do love you," she said, her voice trembling with pained emotion. "I couldn't imagine loving anyone more, even if they were my own flesh and blood."

Resisting the pull of her beckoning arms, he leaned back against the door, allowing his anger to strengthen—his rage to grow.

"You lied to me," he growled, feeling his eyes burn with tears of sadness and fury. "Everything I knew was a lie. How could I even begin to think that what you're saying now is true?"

She began to slowly move toward him, and he waved his arms in an attempt to ward her off.

"Don't!" he yelled, looking away. "Stay where you are."

"I know that I hurt you—and that I don't deserve

your understanding, but you have to know that I want to make it right."

His legs felt suddenly numb, and he slid to floor. She was squatting down beside him now, and he watched with growing horror, powerless to stop her, as she carefully reached a hand out to him.

Tom looked toward the ceiling, knowing that Tremain and his people were watching from a surveillance camera, begging them with his eyes for help.

Her hand touched him, stirring memories of the past, memories that he couldn't be sure were real, but in the end it didn't really seem to matter, because it still hurt like hell.

Tom saw that his mother was looking toward the ceiling as well. "We don't have much time," she said, returning her attention to him.

"Why don't you just leave me alone?" Tom whispered, and with a sudden burst of strength, he pushed himself up from the floor and turned to the door.

He was just about ready to knock when he sensed her behind him. He tensed, as if an electrical shock was coursing through his body, as she wrapped her arms around him and hugged him tightly from behind.

"Whatever happens, I'm doing this for you," she whispered into his ear, and before he could respond, she began to recite something vaguely familiar. "Tyger! Tyger!

Burning bright, in the forest of the night; what immortal hand or eye could frame thy fearful symmetry?"

There was a strange rhythm to way these words were spoken—almost as if they needed to be said in a specific fashion, and by the time Tom realized what was happening, it was too late.

"When the stars threw down their spears and watered heaven with their tears, did he smile his work to see? Did he who made the Lamb make thee?"

Too late.

Victoria Lovett had said something that Tremain couldn't quite make out. "What did she say?" he asked.

On the screen they watched as Tom's body went suddenly rigid and he fell to the floor.

"Holy crap," Mayer blurted.

But Tremain was already on the move, throwing open the door and running toward the stairs. "Get the guards in there now!" he shouted over his shoulder.

I actually started to believe her, Tremain thought, feeling like a fool. He'd actually believed that somehow, somebody like her had been able to reconnect with her humanity after being away from it for so very long.

And it had given him the smallest bit of hope that perhaps, somewhere down the line, there would be a chance for him.

• • •

The three sentries had already gone into the room, weapons drawn.

One of the guards had Victoria Lovett pressed into a corner at gunpoint while the remaining two hovered around Tom, who was sitting limply in one of the interrogation room's chairs.

"What happened, Tom?" Tremain asked as he entered through the open door. He glared at the woman and knelt down beside the young man's chair.

"I blacked out," Tom replied with a shake of his head. He was rubbing the back of his neck as he spoke. "I'm fine, though," he added, and then he smiled. "Think I might still be feeling some of the effects of Dr. Stempler's tests is all."

He stood up, a little unsteady on his feet, and Tremain watched him carefully.

"That poem," Tremain said.

Tom glanced briefly toward the woman. "'The Tyger,'" he said. "It's by William Blake. It's always been one of my favorites." He sighed then, closing his eyes and swaying a little. "I think this has all been just a little too much for me today."

Agent Mayer appeared in the doorway, and Tremain motioned for her to enter.

"Escort Tom to the infirmary and have the doctor

on duty give him a once-over," Tremain said, still keeping a watchful eye on the teen.

"That may not be such a bad idea," Tom agreed.

Tremain paused, searching Tom's face for any sign that something bigger was amiss. He seemed okay, but just in case, since Agent Mayer didn't fully realize what she was dealing with here, Tremain took the agent aside, out of Tom's earshot. "Don't let him out of your sight," he warned.

Mayer gave a quick nod of understanding, then walked over to Tom, who allowed her to take his arm and escort him toward the door.

Tremain watched him go, his heartbeat jumping the tiniest bit when Tom made eye contact with the woman who had pretended to be his mother as he was leaving the interrogation room.

It might have been Tremain's imagination, but he could have sworn that the boy smiled.

They entered the elevator together.

Agent Mayer took the security key from her pocket, slipping the magnetic card into the slot just inside the door. She punched in the floor number to the infirmary as the doors slowly closed.

She'd read the reports, attended the briefings, knew that Tom had been caught up in top secret projects related to Pandora Group since he was young and had recently been faced with the fact that people he believed to be his parents were actually spies. But she still found it impossible to believe that this handsome teenager was anything other than a typical kid as she watched him slump in the corner, hair mussed.

Mayer was reminded of her own son, who was only six but behaved well beyond his years. Her weekend with him was coming up soon, and she made a mental note to do something special with the boy. Kids grew up way too fast.

"Must've been hard," she said, trying to imagine how all the recent traumatic events would affect a kid Tom's age.

"Yeah," he said. His eyes were closed, and he leaned his head back against the elevator wall. "But deep down I always knew I'd get out."

Mayer didn't quite understand. "What was that?" she asked, looking at him quizzically.

Tom chuckled, and for some strange reason she felt the hair on the back of her neck suddenly stand on end.

"He was strong, but I had the patience of a saint."

Mayer still didn't understand. *Why is he speaking like that?* Instinct caused her to move her hand inside her jacket to remove the pistol she had in a shoulder holster beneath her arm.

Tom pushed off the elevator wall in a flash, the palm of his hand lashing out and striking her just beneath her chin. Mayer flew backward, bouncing off the closed elevator doors, her head swimming from the blow. Her hand still fumbled inside her jacket, searching for her gun.

Tom knelt down beside her as the pleasant sound of the elevator chimes filled the air. They had reached their destination.

"He liked you," Tom said, swatting her fumbling hand away and helping himself to her weapon. He took her cell phone as well.

And then it struck her. As she looked up into his handsome teenage face, she realized something wasn't right—he looked different. There was something in his eyes.

"I should put a bullet in your head just for that," he snarled, but instead brought the weapon down viciously, pistol-whipping her.

His eyes are cruel, Agent Mayer thought as the searing agony sank in.

Tom Lovett doesn't have cruel eyes.

Brandon's face hurt where Tyler had punched him. His left eye was swollen shut.

He didn't want his grandmother to see his face, and so he skulked around to the back of the big old house, entering through the servants' door. As quietly as he could manage, he crept into the empty kitchen, breathing a sigh of relief that none of his grandmother's maids were around to see his condition. He didn't trust the women that his grandmother employed; it was like she had eyes and ears all over the house. There wasn't anything he could do that Grandma didn't somehow know about.

He went right to the refrigerator to get some ice, and as he pulled the freezer door open, the wave of chilled air felt pleasant on his throbbing face.

But then he remembered the afternoon's humiliating events, and not even the cold drifting out of the open *freezer could cool the heat of his shame. It had been a few days since he'd last seen Tyler—since his last whupping at the bully's hands—and he had hoped to get home from school again without incident.*

But it wasn't to be.

Tyler had been waiting for him at the end of the winding path through the woods behind the school, the shortcut Brandon used to and from his grandmother's house. He'd thought about turning around and high-tailing it back to the school. Somebody was bound to be there who could help him—old Nick, the janitor, or maybe even Mrs. Benderlake, the geography teacher; she often stayed late after school. But he'd decided against it.

A Kavanagh doesn't run from nobody, *he'd heard his grandmother's shrill voice shriek inside his head. She'd been furious with him after his last encounter with Tyler, not because he'd gotten into a fight and been beaten, but because he had run away.*

Brandon certainly didn't want to get beat up again, but if he ran, Grandma would know, and getting his tail whupped was a whole lot better than that. So, he'd tried to pass Tyler, avoiding his eyes as went. He had always heard that wild animals considered direct eye contact a challenge for their territory, and he'd hoped that maybe that was true of the bully from Plainville.

He wasn't that lucky.

Brandon reached into the freezer, removed one of the metal ice cube trays, and brought it to the sink. He pulled the lever back, releasing the cubes, and dumped most of them into a towel he found on the counter.

No, he wasn't that lucky. But for a moment he'd thought he was, and then he'd heard the movement behind him, turning just in time to meet Tyler's fist with his face. The punch had nearly knocked him out. All he could do was lie on the forest floor, listening to the sound of the bully's laughter as he left him there.

Brandon could still hear the laughing and doubted there would ever be a time when he didn't. He placed the towel filled with ice against his swollen face. At first it hurt like blazes, but gradually he could feel the numbing effects of the cold and the throbbing of his eye starting to subside. Now if he could only get up to his room without Grandma hearing him.

He'd left his schoolbooks on the table, and with one hand holding the ice against his face, he hefted the books with the other and headed through the dining room to the stairs, hoping to get to his room before Grandma woke up from her nap.

But again luck was against him. He tripped on the top step, sprawling to the landing, his books tumbling across the hardwood floor, coming to a stop just in front of Grandma's door.

He lay there perfectly still in the sudden, deafening silence, his heartbeat hammering, hoping that she hadn't heard or, better yet, that she had died in her sleep.

"Brandon, is that you making all that racket out there?" cried a shrill voice from the bedroom. "Come in here, boy."

And as ten-year-old Brandon dragged himself up from the floor of the upstairs hall, he wished himself anywhere other than on his way to see his grandmother.

Even if meant being back on the wooded path on a collision course with Tyler Garrett's fist.

"Dammit," Kavanagh growled, snapping back from yet another bizarre journey to the past.

It was happening more and more frequently these days, and for a moment he seriously considered talking with one of the staff physicians, but then he thought better of it. *A Kavanagh don't show no weakness,* he heard Grandma's ragged voice proclaim, and he shuddered.

"Shut your mouth, you miserable old bat," he growled, stepping out from behind his desk and going to the tiny washroom in his office.

He turned on the cold water in the sink and doused his face liberally, trying to wash away the spiderweb stickiness of the memories. Face dripping, he stared at his reflection in the mirror, briefly seeing himself at age ten—face spattered with blood not his own.

Kavanagh quickly looked away, taking in deep breaths of the stale, recycled air. He wiped his face with a towel and went back to his desk. There were more important things to think about now, things that dealt with the present and his future.

Not the past.

The ringing of his portable phone startled him briefly, but then he glanced at his wristwatch and smiled. "Right on time," he murmured as he picked up the phone from his desk. "Yes?" he questioned, and listened to the response from the familiar voice on the other end.

"Well, hello there, Tyler," he purred into the phone, sitting down on the edge of his desk.

A strange sense of euphoria flowed through him. He would show them; he would show them never to back a Kavanagh into a corner.

Tyger! Tyger! Burning bright, in the forests of the night; what immortal hand or eye could frame thy fearful symmetry?

Tom came awake, the words of William Blake's poetry spoken by Victoria Lovett echoing in his mind. He knew where he was immediately and climbed to his feet, a surge of panic shooting through him like currents of electricity.

He was in the foyer of the old mansion.

"Hello?" he called out, listening for a reply, but all he heard was the haunting sound of the wind blowing outside the old structure.

He walked slowly into the large living room. He remembered the first time he had been here, the first meeting with his doppelganger.

"Are you in here?" he asked the darkened room.

But he knew he was alone; he could feel it. Tyler Garrett wasn't here or anywhere else in the house, so then where . . . ?

The realization struck him like a physical blow. It was what he had feared most since learning of his condition—of his dual personality—and Tom felt his legs go weak as he made his way to one of the sheet-covered sofas.

His mind was racing. *If I'm in here, that means Tyler is out there. How can this have happened?* And then it came back to him: the poem. And he remembered the strange sensation, very much like a narcoleptic attack, as his mother recited the words.

"That bitch!" Tom snapped, launching himself from the sofa and kicking the nearby coffee table, flipping it to its side. "How could I have been so stupid!"

Outside the wind wailed fitfully, and he stopped,

focusing on the sound of the elements, managing to pull back on his rage. The wind seemed to calm. Then he remembered something Tyler had said to him on his first visit—something about this being *his* place; that it responded to his feelings.

"If it's your place," Tom said aloud, looking around the room as the germ of an idea formulated in his head, "and you're me—then it must be my place as well."

He returned to the foyer, stopping near the large winding staircase that led up to the second level. "And this should help me how?" he asked aloud, feeling his frustration rise again.

But he couldn't help it. Just the idea of his alternate self, out there in the real world, inside the Pandora facility, was so terribly disturbing; there was still so much he didn't know about the violent personality that shared his mind. And then he remembered Madison.

"Oh God, oh God," he repeated, pacing around the foyer.

He thought about leaving the mansion, but he had no idea what was outside. For all he knew, it could be some bottomless void that would suck him even deeper into his subconscious.

"Dammit!" he cursed. "I'm the freakin' dominant personality!"

With a renewed determination, he returned to the

spot where he had awakened and dropped to the tiled floor. He made himself comfortable and closed his eyes. Maybe—just maybe—he could wrest control away from Tyler. Using concentration techniques that he'd learned from various doctors to help his narcolepsy, Tom tried to escape the mansion.

He imagined himself deep below the ocean, so far down that the sunlight couldn't even reach him. He was sitting on the sandy bottom, feeling the pressure of the sea all around him, and then he was rising, ever so slowly. The darkness around him started to lighten, the rays of the sun barely permeating the softening gloom as he floated upward. Tom was completely in control, feeling himself emerging from the various layers of unconsciousness that had entwined him.

And still he climbed, turning his face toward the brightening light. Eagerly he kicked toward it—toward consciousness—but suddenly he sensed something in the darkness around him. Below him. He was no longer alone in the lightening ocean of black.

Tom looked down past his feet, at the darkness from which he had emerged and saw that something was following. He suppressed a stab of panic, kicking harder, attempting to ascend faster. The light from above grew brighter, beckoning to him, but the ocean of black had grown suddenly turbulent.

He looked down again to see a shape blacker than the darkness from which it had originated. It was huge—a gigantic beast created to prowl the ocean of his subconscious.

Tom looked into its white, empty eyes, sensing Tyler's involvement.

The shadow beast surged up, its enormous maw opening voraciously wider.

And still Tom tried reaching for the light, striving to awaken. And he was almost there—

But he was taken from beneath, the monstrosity of shadow swallowing him whole in one all-enveloping gulp before beginning its descent back to the inky darkness.

Back to oblivion.

The assassin moved catlike down the corridor, his entire body thrumming with the excitement of being in control again. It felt good to be back, his body whole and not wasting away in some godforsaken dream world.

And then the world tipped suddenly to one side.

"Whoa," Tyler said, losing his balance slightly, bumping up against the wall of the corridor as he made his way to Pandora's information archives. "Not so fast, Tommy," he whispered, allowing the defense mechanisms he'd set up in his mind to kick in.

Tyler had always been planning for a future when he was in control; and being the stickler for detail that he was, he'd planned in advance how to keep his alternate personality locked away where it belonged. The assassin chuckled as the vertigo subsided. Now that he was entirely in the driver's seat, nothing was going to stop him.

Besides, he had a job to do.

As soon as he'd gained control, he'd used Agent Mayer's cell phone to dial a number he'd suddenly remembered. It had turned out to be his boss. At first Tyler had felt a certain amount of resentment toward Brandon Kavanagh, believing that he had been abandoned—cast aside as damaged goods—once the problems with the troublesome Tom Lovett had arisen.

But now he saw that it had all been part of a much bigger plan. He was inside the nerve center of the Pandora Group, right where Kavanagh wanted him to be.

No longer bothered by Tom's attempts to regain control, Tyler continued down the corridor to the archives. He thought about the scene in the interrogation room and almost laughed out loud as he remembered Tremain's concern for his other half. *What happened, Tom?* he had asked, and Tyler had had to bite the inside of his face not to tell him. God, it was hard not to let loose, to eliminate everybody in the room in a matter of seconds as a way of showing that he was back in charge. But he had held himself in check.

Tyler had had no idea that his handler held the key to releasing him from the prison of Tom's mind. *A tiger burning in the night and all.* Who would have guessed it'd be that simple?

He had been so caught up in his thoughts that he didn't even notice the two Pandora agents approaching him until it was too late. They stopped him, one asking where his escort was while the other unclipped a walkie-talkie from the lapel of his jacket and prepared to call in Tyler's infraction.

Tyler couldn't allow that.

He sprang into the air and spun around, the heel of his foot connecting with the chin of the agent who was attempting to reach security. There was a gratifying crack as the man's jaw broke, and he fell to the ground hard.

The other guy had actually managed to draw his gun. He was fast, but Tyler was faster.

The assassin lashed out, bringing his closed fist down on the man's wrist with a sledgehammer-like blow. Again Tyler felt the satisfying sensation of breaking bone as he watched the weapon tumble from the agent's grasp. Then he followed with a blow to the agent's temple, and the man was down before his firearm hit the ground.

Tyler smiled as he surveyed his work. *It's good to be back,* he thought, sprinting down the hallway to the archives. It was only a matter of time before the two agents were discovered. He would have to gather his information quickly and get out before the entire facility was locked down.

He removed Agent Mayer's key from his pocket as he approached the security door, slipped it into the electronic lock, and punched in the entry code that Tom—*he*—had seen the agent use any number of times. The doors opened with a soft hiss and a wave of cool air. The computer room was kept at fifty-five degrees to keep the large CPU, which contained information on every form of technology investigated by Pandora, from overheating. Tyler approached one of the computer stations and sat down in front of the terminal to begin his information extraction. He had to enter Mayer's security code again. Her security clearance wasn't high enough to grant him access to the files he wanted, but it didn't take him long to find a security code that was accepted, as a vision of Tremain pecking at the keyboard just the other day swam in his mind's eye. *Thanks again, Tom.*

"Thatta girl," Tyler said with a coaxing smile as the computer responded, allowing him access to a file called simply *Crypt*. He moved the cursor through the file, searching for a specific name—a Russian name.

The name of a village in Siberia.

"Bingo," he said, opening the document, which

contained all the information Tyler needed about the item named for that Siberian village. "Ain't you the prettiest thing." He chuckled with satisfaction, committing the contents to memory. "And just a road trip away."

The sudden sound of an alarm put an end to his good humor. Quickly he shut down the file and then entered a code of his own, a virus. *This should keep 'em busy for a while,* he thought as he shut down the computer and moved to the door.

He slipped carefully into the hallway, glancing back the way he had come to find the two agents still unconscious on the floor. *They must have found Mayer,* he thought as he turned and headed for the fire stairs at the end of the corridor. No matter—he still had plenty of time to get away.

Victoria Lovett had remained unusually silent since her meeting with the young man she called her son.

Hands bound behind her back as a precaution, they were escorting her to a new holding cell in one of the lower levels of the building. She appeared lost in thought, and Tremain had to wonder what exactly was going through her mind.

The way the boy had reacted, the obvious hurt burning in his gaze. How could anyone live with themselves after being responsible for so much pain? And then the image of his ex-wife standing in the doorway of their bedroom as he packed his suitcase for yet another Pandora operation suddenly filled his mind, the ghostly soft sound of her voice suggesting that it would be best he not return.

I guess it's something you just learn to live with.

He shook himself from his reverie and stepped up beside Victoria, intending to take advantage of her weakness. "You do realize," he said, "that if you remain cooperative, future visits with Tom could—"

Tremain didn't have the chance to finish, for the air was suddenly filled with the sounds of an alarm and an unpleasant, recorded message droning on about a security breach.

He looked at Victoria and caught something in her gaze that told him she knew exactly what was going on.

"What did you do?" he snarled, grabbing hold of her arm and pulling her closer. "What did you do to him?"

The alarms continued their nearly deafening peal as Tyler effortlessly completed climbing the twentieth flight and stopped at a heavy metal door, cursing himself for being a fool.

"What's wrong with you, boy?" he hissed, hand on the cold metal of the doorknob. "You've still got a chance. Slip out through one of the lower levels, help yourself to a fine vehicle, and you're gone. What the hell are you doing?"

Tyler couldn't explain why, but the idea of escaping without Madison Fitzgerald was like leaving a designated target alive after an assassination mission. It was that bad.

It's all his *fault*, Tyler realized, his temper flaring. Since their two personalities had started to merge, certain aspects of Tom's persona had leaked into his own psyche, just as surely as aspects of his own had leaked into Tom's. But now Tom was tucked away where he couldn't do himself or anybody else any harm.

At least that's what Tyler wanted to believe.

Somehow he had picked up Tom's feelings for the girl, and there wasn't anything he could do to shake them. The last thing he needed on this mission was a tagalong, but try as he might, he couldn't wrap his twisted brain around the idea of leaving Madison behind.

For some strange reason, he needed her.

The hell with it; he was running out of time. He would obey his instincts—no matter how stupid they seemed at the moment. He'd just get the girl and leave the facility as quickly as possible. There was still so much he had to do.

He pulled open the door and moved with purpose down the hallway toward Madison's room.

Tyler smiled. The usual guard posted outside the girl's room was nowhere to be seen. *Excellent,* he thought, *maybe this won't be so bad after all.*

And then two agents stepped out of Madison's room. One was Agent Abernathy; the other Tyler didn't recognize. He froze. They hadn't noticed him, but it was only a matter of seconds before they did.

Just enough time.

Keeping his pulse rate steady, he advanced down the hallway, counting the seconds until they saw him.

Abernathy pulled the door closed and was about to say something to his companion when he finally noticed the teen heading toward them. "Freeze, Lovett!" he screamed, drawing his weapon from his shoulder holster.

The other agent reacted as well, jumping back and pulling his own gun. Tyler charged forward. And when they started to fire, he had to wonder if they had been authorized to use lethal force—or if this was something personal.

He drew the weapon he'd taken from Agent Mayer, ready to shoot them both—a head shot for the one he didn't know. He thought he'd be merciful, but Abernathy deserved a whole lot of pain. Tyler had focused down the barrel of the pistol, finger tensing on the trigger, preparing to make his first kill in quite some time, when he realized he couldn't do it.

He couldn't kill.

"Dammit," he spat angrily. It looked like he was going to have to take them down by hand.

He dropped to the ground in a roll and sprang up again between the two agents. Now in danger of hitting each other, they were forced to hold their fire. Still clutching his own gun, Tyler thrust the barrel of the weapon into the unknown agent's throat, the metal jabbing the man's Adam's apple, causing him to stumble back, choking for breath. Abernathy managed to get off a single shot before Tyler was upon him.

"I know how embarrassing it must've been for you to get your ass kicked by a teenager," Tyler said, moving in close.

Abernathy was a fighter; he just wasn't all that good. Tyler was tempted to toy with him for a while, but time was growing too short for fun and games. Instead, he drove his forehead into the agent's chin, pushing him back against the wall. Abernathy was stunned but still tried to raise his weapon. Tyler grabbed his wrist, applying just the right amount of pressure to make him drop the gun and cry out. It was really becoming an old habit between the two of them—Tyler almost wished Abernathy would wise up to the trick just to keep things from getting boring.

"How you gonna explain it this time?" he asked with

a grin, wanting to deliver a killing blow but knocking the man senseless with a succession of three blows to the face.

Abernathy slid down the wall, completely unconscious.

Tyler turned his attention to the other agent. The man was crawling away from him, still gasping for air, one hand clutching his throat while the other reached for a gun that had been dropped in the scuffle.

"You guys just don't learn," Tyler muttered with disgust. Pulling back his leg, he drove the heel of his foot into the back of the agent's neck. The man's head snapped forward and whacked the floor, knocking him out cold.

Sensing more movement behind him, Tyler spun around, believing that Agent Abernathy was tougher than he'd given him credit for, but he realized that it wasn't the agent at all.

Madison Fitzgerald stood in the doorway to her room, mouth agape.

"No time to explain—we have to get out of here," Tyler said breathlessly, doing his best imitation of Tom Lovett.

He held out his hand, and she reached out to take it.

The doctor shone the beam of the tiny flashlight into Agent Mayer's eyes, making sure she was all right.

"And he attacked you—just like that?" Tremain asked. He needed to know everything. Tom had broken into information storage and fought his way out of the facility, Madison Fitzgerald in tow.

Mayer nodded. The doctor handed her a cup of water and some pills. "One minute he was standing at the back of the elevator, very quiet, and the next he was attacking me. I've never seen a kid with that kind of strength before."

Tremain glanced through the window of the examination room to the nurses' station to see that the computer terminals there were still blank. Tom had introduced a virus that had completely shut down Pandora's computer system. The entire network was offline, leaving them without the slightest clue as to where he had gone and what information he had accessed.

"I know I shouldn't have let my guard down," Mayer added with a slight shake of her head. "But he seemed so upset after that scene with his former handler."

Agent Mayer wasn't the only one who'd let her guard down. Tremain himself was well aware of the threat Tom Lovett posed and still found himself feeling sorry for the kid, having developed a completely unprofessional bond. The boy was a weapon, and he should have been treated as such.

The doctor interrupted, telling Mayer that she was free to go but would need a day or so to recuperate. She thanked him, hopping down off the examination table.

"It was almost as if Tom wasn't there anymore," Agent Mayer suddenly said to Tremain as the two left the infirmary.

"What do you mean?" Tremain asked, stopping in the hallway.

"It was like he wasn't Tom anymore—the way he carried himself, the way he moved, even the way he talked."

Only a select few knew Tom's real story. Most of Pandora believed he was simply a troubled youth who had been trained as a double agent by some rogue operatives. It was enough; they didn't need to know the full extent of what had been done to Tom.

"What else?" Tremain demanded, his anxiety rising.

"You should have seen his eyes, sir," Mayer said. She shuddered, pulling her jacket closed and buttoning it. "I've never seen them so cold."

The doctor came out of the infirmary with some paperwork that Mayer had forgotten to sign, and Tremain used the opportunity to excuse himself, quickly heading toward the elevator.

It was time for Victoria Lovett to tell him the truth.

Tom half expected to awaken in the belly of the huge, nightmarish creature that had swallowed him, but instead, he found himself back in the front room of the old mansion.

"I guess this is where you want me to be," he muttered, trying to figure out what he should do next.

The thought of Tyler out there in the real world was almost more than he could stand. He had to do something. He looked toward the stairs and decided that the second floor would be as good a place as any to begin exploring.

Tom started up the winding staircase, noticing as he reached the second floor that the long hallway was lit by gas lamps attached to the wall by tarnished sconces. He didn't remember them being there before. He still found it so hard to believe that none of this was actually real, that the floor beneath his feet, the musty smell of age in the air, the hiss of the gas lamps were all elaborate manifestations of his fractured psyche.

The hallway seemed to stretch for a mile, closed doors on both sides. Slowly he began to walk; then, out of curiosity, he reached out to test one of the doorknobs. It turned easily in his hand, and he pushed the wooden door wider to get a good look at what was behind it.

It was as if the door had opened onto another place entirely. Tom was stunned, stepping back slightly as he peered through to what looked to be a school playground. He listened to the sounds of children playing—some swinging on the swings, others chattering happily as they played on the slide.

At first Tom had no idea what he was watching. But then his brain began to tingle, and he realized that the playground scene unfolding before him seemed strangely . . . familiar.

He stepped farther into the room—onto the playground, the children running around him paying him no mind, as if he wasn't even there, *a ghost*—and he knew that he was in Sweetwater, Texas, at East Ridge Elementary School, where he had attended third grade. . . .

His brain felt like it was moving around inside his skull as he watched a little boy, no older than nine, step from one of the buildings, late for recess because he'd mentioned to his teacher—*Mrs. Fogg, her name was Mrs. Fogg*—that he wasn't feeling well. And after a talk where the good-natured teacher had attempted to discern what was wrong with him, she'd decided that he was fine and sent him out for some sunshine and exercise.

The child was *him*.

Tom remembered the day specifically, knowing what was going to happen. He wanted to call to the younger version of himself, to go to the little boy and tell him not to be afraid.

This was the day—the day he had experienced the first of his narcoleptic attacks.

The wave of vertigo struck unexpectedly, and he thought for sure that he was on the verge of blacking out. The intense dizziness and nausea passed, but something had changed. Tom realized that he was no longer by the open door but across the playground—having become his younger self.

Tom looked down at his hands, marveling at how small they seemed but finding no pleasure in the bizarre experience. He knew what was going to happen and dreaded the feeling of total helplessness that would soon be coming. He braced himself, feeling the strange sensations that he would eventually come to associate with one of his attacks—

And the reality changed again. No longer was he at

East Ridge Elementary. His world had gone cold. He was naked, strapped to some kind of bed, dim circles of light shining down on him from a ceiling above. There was something inside his mouth—something that prevented his teeth from coming together—from biting his tongue.

And two figures, each of them wearing a white lab coat, came to stand above him on either side. He wanted to scream, but the rubber piece in his mouth prevented it.

Where the hell am I? Tom asked himself, returning the stare of the man and the woman.

"I think he's awake," the woman said, stepping closer, reaching down with rubber-gloved hands to pull open one of his eyes. He wanted to slap her rough hands away, but his hands were bound at his sides.

"That's not possible," the man said, adjusting his glasses before he too took a closer look. "My God, you're right."

The two seemed flustered, moving behind a console.

"He's a feisty one. Increase the phenobarb," the man said as the woman acted, and Tom immediately felt his eyes begin to grow heavy. He didn't want to sleep—he wanted to know what the hell was going on.

"Memory implantation should be resuming shortly," the woman said, her voice the last thing Tom heard as his eyes closed and he found himself falling into sleep. "Five . . . four . . . three . . . two . . ."

"Where are we with that?" he heard the man ask, his voice growing farther and farther away.

"He should be at school in Texas, experiencing his first narcoleptic attack."

"Excellent," the man responded. "This should be something that he remembers for the rest of his life."

Tom was in the hallway again, sitting on the floor and staring at the wall where a room used to be. He struggled to his knees, reaching out to touch the firmness of the wall, the peeling wallpaper beneath his fingers.

What's going on? he wondered, recalling it all—East Ridge Elementary as well as the disturbing moments strapped to the table. The room had contained a memory from his past—and something else. He could still taste the foul rubber inside his mouth. That had been a memory too, but one that had not originally belonged to him.

The memory had been Tyler's, and now it was Tom's.

He looked down the corridor at the many other closed doors that awaited him, wondering if behind each of them there existed a moment from the past.

He climbed to his feet and slowly moved to the next door—the mystery of what was hidden behind it and what would be revealed drawing him forward.

•   •   •

It was the third car they had stolen.

Madison walked quickly behind Tom, looking over her shoulder as he picked the latest vehicle. They had been driving for hours, Tom hell-bent on getting them as far away from Washington as he could.

He was being strangely silent. The few times that she had tried to find out what was going on, he'd just given her a look and then told her to trust him.

And how could she do anything but? Tom had saved her life at least twice, and if she thought really hard, she could probably come up with a few more times as well. Madison had to trust him for now, but as soon as she got a chance, she was going to make him tell her what was going on.

They were in another parking garage, this one attached to a mall. They had dumped their last car—a Ford something or other that smelled liked sour milk—in a space on the second level and had taken the stairs up to the fifth to begin their shopping.

Tom stopped near a dark green Subaru Outback, tried the driver's side door, which was locked, but then tried the back door. It opened, and he quickly unlocked the driver's side and then the passenger's so that she could join him.

She thought it would never get old, watching Tom hot-wire a car. It had amazed her when she'd first seen him do it in the driveway of his home, which seemed like a hundred years ago, and it was still something.

He broke the plastic casing over the steering column with a loud crack, and she watched as his fingers deftly sought out the proper wires. In a matter of seconds the car engine turned over and they were ready to get on the move again.

"Tom," she said as he put the car in gear.

It was almost as though he didn't hear her, he was so intensely focused on getting them to where they needed to go. *But where is that?*

She reached out to touch his arm, and he reacted as though she were trying to attack him. He moved lightning fast, slamming the car into park, grabbing her wrist in a grip that she knew could have snapped it like a twig with just the slightest more pressure.

"You're hurting me," Madison said as calmly as she could, even though she was suddenly feeling very *unsafe*. There was a look in his eyes, a dangerous look, and she felt a chill.

He seemed to sense this and smiled. "Sorry," he said, letting her wrist go. "Guess I'm just a little jumpy."

Madison took back her hand, rubbing where he had gripped it so tight, and she continued to watch him—to stare into his eyes.

"What's going on, Tom?" she finally asked. "If you want me to trust you, you have to tell me."

Tom sighed, the muscles in his neck and around his jaw tensing, and he slammed his head back against the headrest. "I found out some things," he said, eyes closed. "From my mother, I found out that Pandora didn't want to help—they wanted to use us." He looked at her then, and she was held by the intensity of his gaze. "They wanted to use me like some kind of secret weapon, but first they had to make me go away."

"I don't understand what you mean," she said.

"They were going to kill me—make me go away so that the other half would be all there was. I couldn't let them do that," he told her with a shake of his head. "I couldn't let them kill me."

It was obvious that he was upset, and she wanted to reach out—to comfort him—but something held her back.

Something still didn't feel right.

"I understand that we had to get out of there, but where are we going now?" Madison asked. "They're part of the government, Tom. How can we get away from the government?"

He smiled at her, and right then she knew what was wrong.

CHAPTER 13

Tremain's head was pounding.

"Explain to me again how he was able to leave the facility with the girl?" he asked Agent Abernathy, whose face looked like twenty miles of bad road after his run-in with the boy. Tremain was certain now that Tom was manifesting the personality of the sleeper assassin, Tyler Garrett.

"We're not sure how exactly, but it was as if he was always one step ahead of us," the man explained.

They were on their way to the holding cells in the subbasement, where Tremain planned to have a long talk with Victoria Lovett. Whatever the woman had done, it had thrown his entire operation into chaos, and he wanted to give a little bit back to her.

"Not sure how he pulled it off?" he asked, his voice sharp with aggravation. "I'll tell you how he pulled it off—he knows exactly how we operate. He's been here for more than two weeks, watching our every move and committing them to memory. He knew we'd do one thing, and he did the other."

Abernathy remained quiet, which was smart. Tremain had heard all about how the agent had attempted to use unauthorized lethal force to stop the boy.

Fat lot of good it did him.

"Anything new on the computer systems?" Tremain asked as they reached the guard stationed just outside the block of holding cells.

"We think we have the bug isolated, and we'll be able to retrieve most of the data soon."

Tremain handed his gun over to the guard for safekeeping. He wasn't taking any chances with this woman.

"I'm going in alone," he said, and then turned back to Abernathy. "If you hear anything about our wayward souls, let me know immediately."

The agent nodded, the dark purple bruises beneath his eyes making him look very much like a raccoon. He seemed about to say something else.

"What is it, Agent?" Tremain asked, trying to keep the impatience from his voice.

"I just want to say how sorry I am that this situation has—"

Tremain stopped him with a hand gesture. "That's enough," he said, proceeding through the door that had been unlocked by the guard. "Let's concentrate on preventing him from making us look like jackasses again."

Victoria Lovett heard the sound of someone approaching and stood, waiting. She breathed a sigh of relief when she saw Director Tremain appear before her cell.

"I can help," she said, stepping closer to the bars.

"Haven't you already done enough?" Tremain asked.

His words were like a physical blow; painfully true, striking deep to her heart. They both knew what she had done to her "son."

"I know what you think of me, but there wasn't a choice," she explained. "If I hadn't triggered the trans-ference, he would have known and—"

"Who would have known?"

"Kavanagh," she replied. "This was all part of his plan: to have Tom brought here, then for me to be cap-tured so that I could be brought here and trigger the change."

"The poem," Tremain stated.

She nodded. "You can't begin to imagine how painful it was for me to speak those words . . . but if I hadn't, he would never have checked in with Kavanagh and been given the specifics of his assignment."

Tremain stepped closer, taking hold of the bars. "Why should I believe you?" he asked. "After all you've done, what makes you think that anything you say could bear any weight?"

"Because if I hadn't done what I did, Brandon Kavanagh would be on the move again, disappearing from the face of the earth to plan some other terrible way to get even with Pandora for throwing a wrench into his plans."

"Well, if that's true, why didn't you tell me what you were up to right away and where Kavanagh is? Why the secrets?"

She paused. "Maybe I don't trust *you*," she replied. "I had to follow this through because it's the best thing for Tom. I wasn't sure you would have allowed me to do it my way. In fact, I'm sure you wouldn't have."

The director remained silent.

"As of now, Kavanagh believes that everything is going according to plan," she added.

"And do you know what that plan is?"

She moved closer, the two of them separated only by the metal bars of the jail cell. "Not everything, but I managed to piece together some basic intel from our conversations. The rest I got from reading notes scrawled on pieces of paper on his desk and snippets of phone conversations I overheard when I was coming and going from his office."

"Do you know where Tom . . . *Tyler* is going?"

"I want to be involved," she stated.

Tremain shook his head. "That's out of the question."

Victoria backed away from the bars and returned to her cot.

"There are other ways I can get this information from you," Tremain threatened.

She looked up at him. "I want to help you—just let me be a part of this operation, and I'll tell you everything I know."

Tremain turned and walked away from the room.

Victoria felt her resolve begin to crumble; she couldn't do anything from inside this cell. She was starting to consider alternatives to the offer she'd made Tremain when she heard the sounds of feet coming down the hall.

Pandora's director had returned with her jailer. The man unlocked the door, allowing it to swing wide, and Tremain moved to stand in the entryway.

"Do we have a deal?" she asked, still not moving from her cot.

Tremain nodded. "But give me one more reason to

suspect betrayal"—his eyes became incredibly dark—and I'll kill you in an instant."

She rose, walking to stand before him.

"Fair enough," she agreed.

Tyler didn't require sleep; well, not in the usual sense of the word.

His brain was set up in such a way that he could appear wide awake while sections of his mind were actually shut down, recharging. And that was what he was doing as they drove down I-70, the highway flying past on either side of them.

Madison moaned softly in the seat beside him. She'd been awake for most of the trip, finally succumbing to sleep just a few hours ago. He knew that she suspected who he really was. He also knew that she could be a liability, but he just didn't care. For a reason he had yet to fully understand, Tyler needed her with him. If a problem arose, he would have to deal with it, but until then he wanted Madison by his side.

His thoughts were suddenly filled with memories of when they'd first met; an image of her walking away from him across his yard burned into his mind.

His memories.

Tyler snapped from the recollection. He was furious, wanting to strike out at something—to drive his fist into soft flesh, feeling the fragile bones beneath collapse against his onslaught.

Pulling the car over to the side of the road, Tyler sat rigid, gripping the steering wheel tightly in both hands. There were more memories now, moments of a mundane existence that suddenly belonged to him.

"What are you doing?" he growled.

"What's wrong?" Madison asked groggily beside him, coming awake with a start.

He wanted to tell her that everything was fine, that he had everything under control.

But Tyler knew he would have been lying.

How many doors had he torn open in the seemingly endless upstairs corridor? Behind each and every one existed a memory, some true, others . . . not his own.

Tom had almost fallen to his knees again in one of the memory rooms, hanging on to the doorknob, still awash in the warm recollection of the first time he'd really *seen* Madison Fitzgerald. They had been talking, getting to know each other, and then it was time for her to go. He hit the instant-replay button inside his head, watching as she walked across the yard to the fence.

He found himself in the hallway again, standing in front of a section of wall where a room had once been. It was the same thing over and over: open a door and release a memory. A part of him was afraid of what he would find behind each door, but another reveled in it. Tom knew that this was where he would find the answers to the questions that haunted him.

Who am I? Who is Tom Lovett really? Does he actually exist, or was he, too, created by scientists in some secret lab?

Tom turned and looked down the endless corridor. Many doors had yet to be opened.

So many memories to be recalled, so many still to be experienced.

There wasn't any time to waste.

It was cold in the desert, and Kavanagh wished he had brought along a jacket, but the invigorating chill of the desert winds reminded him that he was still alive.

He had adopted this as a nightly ritual, a way to escape the stale, recycled air of the underground installation that had become his newest base of operations. Every night he would ride the elevator up from the bowels of the earth and emerge from the abandoned military base to breathe the fresh air and look at the stars. Tonight Noah Wells accompanied him, and they stood outside the building that had once housed the commissary, the stink of Well's cigarette tainting the air.

Kavanagh squinted against the biting chill, turning his head slightly. He watched as Wells puffed his cigarette, taking the full brunt of the cold desert air, tears running down his gaunt face.

"You're crying," Kavanagh said as he crossed his arms in an attempt to keep warm.

Wells reached up, touching the moisture that ran from his eyes and down his cheek. He didn't feel it or the bite of the desert wind.

"Must be cold," he said, staring at the moisture that dampened his fingertips. "Do you want to go back down?"

Kavanagh shook his head and looked up into the night sky. "Not yet," he said, dreading the return underground. A part of him wished he could disappear right then, get into a car and drive away, leave it all behind. But he knew he couldn't do that—a Kavanagh never ran away from his problems.

And besides, he didn't believe in failure. Something could always be done to turn a situation around; his grandmother had taught him that, miserable witch that she was. She'd taught him to never lie down, to never accept that he'd been beaten, and if he was, to take as many down with him as he could.

"Come on in here, boy," Grandma ordered, *and Brandon felt the world drop out from under him.*

Her bedroom stank of Lysol and something else, a stink so pervasive that not even the powerful disinfectant could wash it completely away. Every time Brandon smelled it, he wanted to gag.

The room was dark, illuminated only by a single beam of sunlight that had managed to find its way through a slight part in the thick curtains covering the large windows. His eyes started to adjust to gloom, and he could just about make out the shape of his grandmother's large four-poster bed in the center of the room. He was looking for her, and his heart skipped a beat as his gaze fell on the wheelchair beside the bed—but it was a false alarm; the chair was empty.

"It's always something," came his grandmother's voice, and a shape that he had mistaken for bedclothes rose up on the bed. "An old gal can't even get the proper rest she needs to live a long and healthy life."

She tossed the blankets aside and pushed herself up into a sitting position. Brandon couldn't help but think of the scarecrow in Mr. Stanley's field—the sharp angles of its framework beneath the old clothes it wore. His grandmother was nothing more than skin and bones. Many times he had overheard the hired help wondering how it was that she was even still alive.

But she was, and he had regretted it pretty much every day since the death of his parents, when she had become his guardian. The old woman positioned herself at the edge of the big bed, reaching out to pull the wheelchair closer. She stood momentarily on spindly legs before dropping down into the seat.

"Come over here, boy," Grandma spat as she grabbed her cane from where it hung on one of the bedposts. Even though she mostly used the wheelchair these days, she seldom went anywhere without her cane. It had belonged to Brandon's grandfather. He had carved it with his own two hands from a solid branch of maple, brought down by a bolt of lightning in the summer of 1922—at least that was what she told him. Brandon imagined that she kept it around as a reminder of her dead husband but also as means to make certain her points were heard and understood.

Brandon slowly moved closer, trying to sidestep the beam of sunlight. He could actually feel her eyes on him— like two fat horseflies crawling over his face—and suddenly he had to go to the bathroom worse than he could ever remember.

"Did somebody beat you up again, Brandon?" she asked with a disappointed shake of her head. "I may be old, but I ain't blind."

His eyes darted about the room, looking everywhere but at her.

"Look at me when I'm talking to you!" she shrieked,

and the cane was suddenly lashing out at the side of his leg.

It connected with a loud crack, and Brandon recoiled, pulling his hurt leg up and balancing on the other. He looked at his grandmother, the almost-translucent quality of her skin pulled tightly around her skull, what little hair she had left like balls of cotton glued to pig hide. Brandon couldn't help but think of the pictures of Egyptian mummies he had seen in National Geographic.

"Still that same brat that moved here from Plainville last summer?" she asked him. "The one that left you cryin' like a little girl?"

"Yes, ma'am," he said quickly, not wanting to feel the bite of her cane again. "It was the same boy that done this."

With a hand gnarled by rheumatism she reached out and grabbed hold of his face, turning it toward the sunlight. "That eye's a sin," she hissed, giving his face a shake before letting it go. "Did you at least fight back this time?"

Brandon lowered his gaze. It was pointless to fight back against Tyler Garrett—no matter how hard he hit, Tyler hit back four times as hard, and Brandon was truly afraid that the bully would kill him one of these days.

"Guess that answers my question. You remember what I said to you last time?"

Brendan nodded. "I was listening. There's just nothing I can do; he's bigger than me and . . ."

The old woman leaned forward in her seat, resembling a

buzzard waiting for its prey. "Then you go after him first for a change—hurt him bad, make it so he learns to be afraid a ya."

Grandma suddenly raised her cane again as if to strike him, and Brandon flinched, covering his face in fear.

She laughed, a horrible wet-sounding cackle, as she lowered her weapon. "See how it works?" she asked.

She was silent for a long time. "Fear has become your master. You're like one of them fancy poodle dogs at the end of its leash."

Grandma started to cough, a horrible hacking, barking sound, and by the way her body trembled and shook, he thought for sure she was going to break her brittle old bones with the powerful force of her coughs.

Brandon stepped closer. "Are . . . are you all right, Grandma?"

The coughing stopped, and she slumped to one side a bit in the wheelchair. She lifted a spidery hand to her skeletal face and wiped away a bead of spittle that threatened to fall from end of her lip.

"What's the matter, boy?" she asked breathlessly. "Scared that your grandma's gonna die?" She leaned forward again, her cadaverous face no more than two inches from his. "You're a Kavanagh, Brandon," she snarled. "That don't mean much to you now, but it will someday. We don't let fear rule us—you understand me? We take

fear by the scruff of its neck and we make it work for us."
She pretended to be holding something in her twisted hand
in front of his face. "See here?" she asked. "I got me some
fear right here in my hand."

He'd started to shake, her words slowly sinking in.

"And if I felt like it, I could use this fear to get what-
ever I want. Fear is a powerful tool, Brandon Kavanagh."

He nodded, finally understanding what it was she was
trying to tell him.

Grandma lifted her prized cane from her lap and
shoved it at him.

"Hold that," she barked, and he did, feeling the smooth,
polished wood in his hands.

"Now you got some fear in your hands too," she said, a
cruel smile playing at the corners of her mouth. "What are
you gonna do with it?"

"I think it's time we went back down," Noah Wells
said, his voice bringing Kavanagh back from the past.

He looked around—at the nighttime sky and the
remnants of the base, as if seeing it for the first time.

With fresh eyes.

"You're right," he said, walking back toward the
commissary and the secret elevator that would take
them back to the installation hidden deep beneath the
earth.

Soon he would have fear in his hands—the kind of fear that could make a man extremely powerful.

What are you gonna do with it? he heard his grandmother ask.

And as before, he knew exactly what to do.

Victoria hadn't known the specifics of Tyler's mission, but what she did know gave Tremain enough information to fill in the blanks, and suddenly it all made a twisted kind of sense. He'd never wanted a drink so badly in his life.

He entered the briefing room, where his staff of operatives waited, tired and bleary-eyed from lack of sleep. In the corner he saw Victoria Lovett and, sitting inconspicuously near her, Agent Mayer. She knew what the situation required if necessary.

Tremain looked at each and every one of them, struggling with the information that he possessed and wondering exactly how much he should share. He'd already been forced to give them the truth about what Tom really was. With the boy changed and in the outside world, he couldn't afford any more mistakes in tracking him down.

"You're all aware of Tom Lovett's unique condition,"

he began without preamble. "I believe I know now why Brandon Kavanagh wanted his change triggered."

"Do you know where he's headed, sir?" asked Agent Abernathy from his seat at the conference table.

Tremain felt a cold fear in his chest. "I believe I do," he said, taking a deep breath.

"Are any of you familiar with the Crypt?"

"Is this where we're going?" Madison asked, breaking the silence that had filled the car since she'd woken up.

They were in Oregon, and as they passed a sign that announced Crichton Falls, Tyler seemed to grow more restless, tapping his fingers on the steering wheel.

He took his eyes off the road to stare at her, and she had to fight not to look away. She wasn't sure if he knew she suspected that he wasn't who he said he was. How on earth would he react if he realized it for certain?

"Not quite," he said, putting his eyes back on the road.

Madison breathed a sigh of relief. His stare made her skin crawl. She had never wanted to see Tom more than when this stranger in his body looked at her. It was the wildest thing—to anybody else she would guess that he looked exactly like Tom Lovett, and for all intents and purposes, he was. But she knew otherwise. Tom

Lovett wasn't here right now. This guy—this Tyler Garrett—was just wearing a mask.

"What we're looking for is on the outskirts." He smiled, his fingers tapping the steering wheel to the beat of some tune that only he could hear. "Don't worry, we'll be there soon enough."

Which was exactly what she was afraid of. She'd thought about trying to escape earlier, but one look into his eyes had told her that she wasn't likely to get very far. And besides, what would happen to Tom if she left? Some instinct deep inside told her that if anyone could help Tom come back to the surface and fight off Tyler, it was her. She knew she could get through to him if she just had the chance. So she'd decided to wait and to watch, hoping for some kind of opportunity to present itself.

They drove through Crichton Falls. It was a cloudy morning, and the town looked like a very depressing place. The houses were run-down, as though they hadn't been taken care of in years: peeling paint, broken windows, sagging front porches. And she didn't see a soul. Madison was beginning to wonder if anyone actually lived in Crichton Falls when she saw the sign. She craned her neck, trying to read it as they passed, but all she could make out were the words *No Trespassing* and *Environmental Protection Agency*.

"Did you see that?" she asked Tyler.

"I did," he answered, slowing down to head left at a fork in the road.

"So this town is abandoned?"

"Yep," he said, speeding up on the twisting length of road. "The residents were relocated after the EPA found that their groundwater had been contaminated by a toxic waste containment facility nearby."

Madison held on to the car door as Tyler navigated the winding course to their destination. "So the EPA just moved the whole town out?"

"They did," Tyler said, "and then they gave the cleanup contract to a company called Enviro-Safe."

"So what happened?" Madison questioned as they came around a bend to find the road blocked by a high fence, topped with barbed wire.

Tyler stopped the car and turned off the engine. "Enviro-Safe said that Crichton Falls was too badly poisoned and that no amount of cleanup could ever make the place safe." He smiled at her again, and she felt her skin crawl. "It was a lie."

Tyler opened the car door and climbed out.

"Wait," she called, getting out of the car as well. "Why would they lie?" It was a relief just to escape the confines of the car, even though she knew there was no getting away from Tyler.

"Enviro-Safe was a cover for the Pandora Group,"

he said casually, assessing the fence. "They saw the perfect opportunity here and decided to claim the land as their own."

Tyler walked back to the car, flicking a switch that opened the rear of the Outback. He pulled out a heavy blanket.

"I don't get it. Why would Pandora want a bunch of land poisoned by toxic waste?" Madison asked.

"It's the perfect cover," he explained, starting to climb the fence, blanket in hand. "An entire area that everybody is afraid of—that people stay away from. It's the perfect place for them to store their own brand of toxic waste."

He tossed the blanket over the wire, covering up a section of its razor-sharp barbs, and dropped back down to the ground beside her.

"After you," he said, motioning toward the fence.

"You want me to climb?"

"It's the only way we're going to get in."

"We're going in there?" She peered through the chain-link fence up the road at the shape of the abandoned factory squatting in the distance.

He grabbed her arm. "Climb," he ordered.

She thought about arguing but instead did as she was told, slowly making her way up. Tyler was right behind her, helping her to make it over the blanket. She dropped down on the other side of the fence, and he landed in a crouch, catlike, beside her.

He started toward the building.

"I thought you said there was toxic stuff up there," she said, holding back.

He turned back to her. "Not actual toxic waste. Things that Pandora has acquired over the years but deemed so dangerous they had to be hidden away—stored deep underground where they couldn't hurt anybody."

Madison suddenly felt herself growing very afraid. "But why are we here?" she asked, her eyes glued to the dark, foreboding facade of the facility.

"We're going shopping," Tyler said, taking hold of her arm and pulling her along.

Tom stopped at the edge of the shadow.

He had continued down the seemingly endless corridor, opening door after door and immersing himself in moments of memory, fragments of a childhood that defined him as the person he was now and others that showed exactly how a killer was made. From learning how to ride a two-wheeler to making explosives with items found in a typical kitchen, as soon as the doors were opened, the memories belonged to him.

The corridor was growing darker. The shadows

seemed unusually dense here, the very atmosphere thick with something that made him jittery.

Tom stopped at a discernable line of shadow, trying to see farther down the hall into the swirling murk. There were more doors on both sides of the corridor, but there was also something else. He squinted, curious to see what awaited him, and stepped into the thickening shadow. It was as if he was wrapped in a blanket of cold mist, the shadow seeming to converge on him—to embrace him—but he continued forward, barely able to make out the shape of something ahead.

At first he couldn't believe his eyes. He'd been traveling this upstairs hall for what seemed like days, and what appeared through the shifting clouds of shadow at the end of the hallway was another door, but this one—this one was different.

The darkness swirled, and he found himself becoming colder, rubbing vigorously at his arms and chest, trying to get the blood circulating as he continued on. It was almost as if he were drawn to it—a supernatural current pulling him along. He wondered briefly about the other doors he passed, but he couldn't take his focus from the door ahead. It was as if the darkness didn't want him to see it, blowing thickly like smoke, trying to hide it from his sight.

Too late.

The door was large and appeared to be made of tarnished metal. It reminded him of one of those huge bank vault doors in the movies, completely out of place in the hallway of a run-down mansion. The closer he got to it, the farther away it seemed to become, but that just intensified his desire to reach it. There was a breeze in the hallway now, moving the darkness like a fog, attempting to push him back, but he continued forward, planting each foot solidly on the floor, inexorably moving closer.

Tom reached a point where he thought he could almost touch it and extended his arm and then his fingers—the tip of his index finger almost connecting with the hard, dirty surface.

"What the hell do you think you're doing?" asked a voice from somewhere in the shadows, and he pulled back his hand, whirling around, heart racing with terror as he realized he was no longer alone.

"I suggest you come away from there right now before you hurt yourself," the voice commanded.

It seemed to be coming from all around, and as Tom searched for its source, he realized that he knew this voice.

"Have you done your homework yet?" it asked. "I'm free right now if you want help with that geometry assignment."

It was the voice of his father.

"I was . . . I was just looking at this door," Tom

explained, moving away from it toward the voice, the unnatural wind at his back assisting him.

"Well, come away from it," the voice ordered. "There's still a lot to be done tonight before you can goof off."

Tom thought he'd figured out where the voice had come from and was focusing his eyes on a particular area of darkness when he felt the pull. It was as if somebody had tied a rope around his waist and was pulling him backward. The door was pulling him toward it again. He turned, seeing it as if for the first time, partially hidden behind veils of swirling black, and again felt the compulsion to touch it.

"Tom, didn't you hear what I said?" his father bellowed.

He cringed at the sound of anger in his father's voice. It took a lot to make him that mad; his dad very seldom raised his voice.

"Your mother and I have been very concerned about you," his father said. "You've seemed distracted, as if there's something on your mind."

Your mother and I. The words were like shards of glass rubbed into his chest.

"You're not my father," he yelled into the darkness as he turned away from the door.

Something shifted, a figure blacker than the darkness

around it. It disengaged itself from the shadows and moved toward him.

Tom felt a trembling weakness in his legs, and a scream tried to slither up his throat as his father came into view. The man had been burnt, and there was nothing to distinguish him as Tom's father other than the dark green cotton shirt and chinos he had been wearing the last time Tom had seen him—when the two had fought and the man had tried to kill him.

There also had been explosions that day—two houses blown to bits. Tom remembered the searing flash and the sound of every bad thunderstorm he could remember all rolled into one as the houses were obliterated. He had escaped—it didn't look like his dad had been so lucky.

He was practically a skeleton; what might have been charred pieces of skin drifted gently down from his body like flakes of black snow. But his clothes appeared fine.

Nightmares are funny that way.

"How could you say such a thing?" Mason Lovett asked—sounding far better than he should have in his condition. "I think it's time that the two of us sat down and had a long talk about your attitude." He extended a blackened hand. "C'mon, son, let's have ourselves a little chat about the future—about *your* future."

Tom stumbled back, away from the hand and closer to the door.

"Get away from that goddamned door!" Mason screamed, and lunged, grabbing hold of the front of Tom's T-shirt, trying to pull him from the door. "You've become a different person, Tom," Mason Lovett's burnt corpse scolded.

"I *am* different," Tom found himself saying. He grabbed the man's wrist and twisted it, forcing it to release its grip on his shirt. "And don't touch me again," he told the corpse as he shoved it away from him.

"Ever."

The charred version of Mason stumbled backward, then reached behind him and pulled out a glinting butcher knife. "I've had just about enough of your bad attitude, young man."

Haven't we done this already? Tom thought, his body immediately tensing as the corpse lunged at him, the knife blade aimed at his heart.

Tom sidestepped the thrust, grabbing hold of the arm in one hand and in one fluid move bringing the elbow of his other arm down onto Mason's. There was a loud snap followed by a shrill scream as the arm was broken, the knife clattering to the floor.

Tom squatted down, reaching for the fallen blade, but his father lashed out, kicking him in the face and causing him to fall backward.

"Don't know what could've gotten into you," Mason

grumbled, reaching down to retrieve the knife with his good hand while the other dangled uselessly at his side. "But I'm going to do my damnedest to make sure I cut it out."

Tom was nearly on his feet when Mason attacked again. Tom tried to avoid the slashing blade, but he didn't move fast enough. The butcher knife sliced a gash through the front of his shirt and across the tight muscles of his abdomen beneath. The wound burned like fire as he jumped back. Tom touched his stomach, his hands coming away stained red.

"That'll teach you to talk back to your father," the corpse said, its features twisted in a disturbing attempt at a smile.

Mason charged at him again, and Tom felt his anger explode. He sprang off from the ground, his shoulder connecting with his father's midsection and driving him back, the tip of Mason's knife glancing off Tom's shoulder as the two landed on the floor in a struggling heap.

"You're in for it now, mister," Mason roared, attempting to plunge the blade into his son's throat.

Tom turned away, managing to avoid its bite. "I've had enough of this," he growled, wrenching the knife from the corpse's hand, flipping it deftly in one hand, catching it, and driving it down through his father's chest.

Mason screamed—a disturbing, high-pitched cry—

as he tried to pull the knife from his chest. Tom stood, staring for a moment at the hideous scene before him, then turned back to the door.

The shadows parted again to reveal the metal obstruction. It seemed larger than before as he slowly approached it. Tom reached out, laying his hands on its surface. He expected it to be cold beneath his touch but instead found it comfortingly warm.

He stepped back, studying the hard metal surface, trying to determine how to open it.

"I'm going to be very angry with you!" Mason's voice slurred behind him. "Go through that door and things will never be the same."

"Shut up," Tom snarled, again pressing his hands to the door's warm surface.

"Don't you talk to me like that!" Mason screamed. "I don't care what you think, but I'm still your father and—"

Tom couldn't control it anymore, suddenly lashing out at the metal door. "You're not my father!" he bellowed, pounding his fist down on the hard surface.

The door shook with the force of the blow, and bits of plaster rained down from around the frame. Tom stepped back, surprised by his sudden strength.

"Listen to me," his father begged. "It can be like it was before. Wouldn't you like that, Tommy?"

Tom pounded on the door again, his anger seeming to flow through his body, escaping from his fists as he beat on the metal obstruction. "It was all a lie," he said, hitting the door again and again.

He paused momentarily. The door was dented, and he felt the strength surge through his body, sensing that one more strike would bring it crashing down.

"Don't do it!" his father warned, pushing himself up on his one good arm. "I guarantee you won't like what you'll find."

"I'll just have to take that chance," Tom said, and brought his fist down into the center of the door.

He watched, stunned, as the twisted metal fell forward through the frame, tumbling down into a sea of darkness below. The pull on Tom began to intensify. For a moment he fought it, straining the muscles in his upper body as he tried to force himself back from the edge of the precipice, but then he came to the frightening realization that that was where he needed to go.

"Tommy, don't," his father croaked, reaching out to him with a blackened, skeletal hand.

But Tom closed his eyes, resisting the pull of the darkness no longer, allowing himself to be drawn over the edge.

Falling into oblivion.

CHAPTER 15

Madison had never really thought of herself as claustrophobic, but she was seriously considering the possibility as she slowly backed her way down through the narrow metal shaft.

The Enviro-Safe facility had been locked up tight, not a door to pick the lock on or a window to break, and part of her had breathed a sigh of relief, thinking that maybe, just maybe, Tyler would give up and they'd leave.

"How are we doing?" he asked from in front of her, and she almost told him to kill the sweet act, but she held her tongue.

"I'm good," she answered instead, concentrating on not losing her traction. The shaft was slick with the residue of a grainy substance.

They must have been looking for over an hour,

examining every nook and cranny, trying to find a way in. They had finally found a section at the far back of the building, near what looked to be loading docks, where the siding came away to reveal a square metal hatch attached with clamps. Within seconds Tyler had removed all four of the clamps and discarded the cover, telling her to crawl inside.

She hadn't argued with him; there was a look in his eyes and a tone in his voice that said it wouldn't have been in her—*or Tom's*—best interests. Tyler had been acting weirder by the minute, at times going strangely quiet, as if listening to something that only he could hear.

It kind of freaked her out. Almost as much as climbing down a greasy metal shaft into a top secret government facility. Almost.

She brought a hand to her face, sniffing the odd substance coating the sides of the shaft. It wasn't a bad smell, reminding her strangely enough of potatoes. She came to the realization that this gritty substance wasn't the residue of anything mechanical.

"Crumbs," she said aloud.

"What?" Tyler asked.

"This stuff—in the chute here—it's like cookie—"

And then suddenly there was a shriek of bending metal, and Madison felt the support beneath her give way. The shaft broke and she tumbled out, hitting the ground hard and knocking the wind from her lungs.

She just lay there for a moment, her body thrumming with the shock of the fall. Slowly she began moving her arms and legs to be sure there were no broken bones. Everything seemed all right, and she rolled onto her hands and knees in time to see Tyler drop down from an open area of wall where the chute had once been attached.

"Are you okay?" he asked, feigning concern as he lowered himself silently to the floor.

"I'm just fine," she snapped back. Madison brushed away the oily crumbs from her clothes as Tyler walked around the small room in which they now found themselves.

"What were you saying before?" he asked. He was standing in front of a gray square box, positioned directly below where she had fallen.

"I said the stuff that was coating the shaft—that's all over us?" She showed him her fingers and then brushed them off. "It's like cookie crumbs or something."

"I think you're right," he said, moving closer to the box and hitting a circular red button. There was a slight hum, and four cookielike objects dropped down into a basin beneath the opening. Tyler picked up one of the biscuits and smelled it.

"Smells like a potato," he said with the slightest hint of a twang, and she felt her pulse rate flutter.

He dropped the unappetizing-looking snack to the floor. "Some kind of distribution source for food, looks like." He walked around the box. "Over here there's a spigot for water."

She watched as he put his hand beneath one of the metal tubes protruding from the body of the box, his hand coming away wet. Tyler's eyes darted around the room, checking out every shadowy corner.

"Why would food and water be here?" she asked him. "I thought you said this was some kind of storage place."

Tyler said nothing, heading toward a door.

"Hey," she called, following him. "I asked you a question."

"Let's just find what we came for and get out of here," he said gruffly.

"And just what is that?" she asked him. "I know I've asked you this a million times since we left Washington, but why did we come all this way?"

He stopped and glared, and for a minute she thought that he might just hit her. But then his expression softened.

"Things aren't the way you think they are," he told her.

You got that right, Madison thought.

"But I think that once we get what we came for here, it'll all start to make sense."

There was a desperation to his look, as if he actually wanted to believe the crap he was shoveling. Something was definitely wrong with Tom's other personality, and she had to wonder—*had to hope*—that Tom might have something to do with it.

She nodded, seeming to accept what he said, and continued down the hallway beside him. A few feet down, it opened up into a huge warehouse space, filled with storage containers of all sizes and shapes, some plain wooden crates and others more modern, like futuristic pieces of luggage.

She slowed down, taking it all in. Almost every corner of the huge room was filled with some kind of box, crate, or container. There was stenciled writing on some of the boxes that she couldn't quite make out and symbols on others. Madison saw the symbol for radiation on quite a few of the more modern, plastic cases.

She jumped as Tyler's hand touched her shoulder.

"Are these all weapons?" she asked him.

"Most, I guess," Tyler answered. "All the stuff Pandora doesn't want falling into the wrong hands."

"There's so much of it," she said, allowing herself to be led from the room.

"And this is only the tip of the iceberg," he told her as they passed through yet another doorway into an even larger room, this one filled with all kinds of vehicles. There were trucks and airplanes and even what looked to be a submarine hanging from a heavy-duty harness attached to rigging in the ceiling.

Her head was spinning. The facility was enormous, seeming to go on forever, room after room of items capable of who knew what, stored beneath the ground in Oregon. Man, this world just kept getting weirder and weirder.

How can I ever look at it the same way again?

They found themselves in another sparsely lit corridor, descending to a high-tech security door. Tyler approached the keypad lock at the side of the door and punched in a numbered code.

"You'd think they would have changed the combination after all this time," he said as a light began to flash red, bathing the hallway a sickly pink shade as the metal door slid open with a hiss. "But then again, this is the government we're talking about." He smiled and stepped through the doorway into another short corridor that led to yet another room. "If it ain't broke, don't fix it."

A large, thick-paned window to the side of the door gave them a view of the room's contents: row after row of metal shelving containing canisters that reminded her of the thermos her father took to work with him every day.

Madison thought of her parents again, wondering how they were and wishing that she was with them. But then Tyler had the door open after punching in another number code on a keypad and was pushing her out of the way. She followed him in, the door sliding closed behind her. She watched as he moved up and down the rows, carefully examining the canisters.

It was freezing inside, and goose bumps erupted across the surface of her flesh. She stopped to read the words stenciled on a row of canisters.

Pasteurella pestis.

There were other words too, but these were the ones that stood out. She knew these words. Madison recalled junior-year biology, when Mr. Divirgilio had spent at least a week teaching them about a period during the late Middle Ages when one-third of the English population had died because of plague—the Black Death.

"Oh my God," she whispered.

"What's wrong?" Tyler asked, one of the silver containers tucked beneath his arm.

"These are all diseases, aren't they?" She looked around the room.

"They certainly are," he said. "Those things stored

out there"—he hooked a thumb in the direction of the outside rooms—"they're like sticks and stones compared to the killing power kept in here."

She stared at the canister he was holding. "What are you going to do with that?"

Tyler plucked it from beneath his arm. "This one was discovered in Siberia—at a secret Russian biological research station. Death's Kiss 75," he said with a certain amount of awe. "Supposedly it killed every single person in the station as well as the village before going dormant in the cold. Can you imagine?" Madison didn't respond. "What do you think I'm going to do with it?" he said finally, giving her a blood-freezing smile.

Madison blinked. This was it—he wasn't hiding it anymore, the fact that he was Tyler, not Tom. And if he didn't feel like he had to pretend, that was a very bad sign. . . .

He strode toward the exit.

"No," she said, following.

"No?" he repeated, glancing over his shoulder. "I wasn't asking for permission, honey."

Without hesitation Madison pulled Tyler's shoulder back and grabbed at the canister.

"I won't let you leave with that," she said, her fingers glancing across the metal surface.

Tyler turned and slapped her across the face, sending her stumbling back onto the floor. She saw stars momentarily as her mouth filled with the coppery taste of blood.

Tyler was staring at his hand as if it wasn't his own.

"If I can't stop you," she said, wiping away the blood dripping from her lip, "*Tom* will."

Tyler gazed at her for a moment, his hand clutching the canister so tightly his knuckles were white. He quickly turned away from her, tucking the canister under his arm. He pushed a button on the wall, opening the door of the freezing room.

She was right behind him as he stormed up the incline toward the warehouse rooms. "He's still in there, isn't he?" she said. "Somehow he's locked up inside, and I bet he's fighting to get out."

"I'd shut up if I were you," Tyler snarled, not turning around.

It was clear to Madison that she was getting to him. "Do you think he can hear me? If I tried to talk to him, do you think he would hear and try to take over?"

Tyler spun around, a menacing glint in his eyes. "If I have my way, he ain't never comin' back, darlin'," he growled, bearing down on her.

As he leaned in close, Madison lunged, snatching the canister away.

"You little bi—" Tyler began, but she was already running.

She was halfway through the storage room filled with crates when she saw movement from the corner of her eye. Thinking that somehow Tyler had managed to get ahead of her, Madison stopped, eyes searching the room, trying to find another way out. But it wasn't Tyler.

Whatever it was, it moved incredibly fast, springing from box to box, disappearing in patches of shadow only to emerge again in a flurry of blurred movement. It finally stopped, perched on a nearby stack of crates, staring at her with glowing red eyes. Madison held her breath, terrified. At first glance it appeared to be some kind of machine—a robot, maybe—but as she watched it move, she came to the horrifying realization that there was something flesh and blood beneath the metal covering.

And then it sprang from its perch, landing in a clattering crouch, its metal claws clicking across the hard surface as it charged, an echoing roar issuing from its fanged mouth.

At one time, it might have been some kind of monkey, she thought as it leapt at her.

Tyler felt like an idiot.

His head was swimming as he chased her through the warehouse.

He was getting sloppy, and he blamed it on the gradual merger of his and Tom Lovett's personalities. Mr. Kavanagh had said that he could make Tom Lovett go away forever. For that, Tyler would have destroyed the world, and who knew, maybe releasing the Kamchatka virus would do just that. But it didn't matter as long as he didn't have to return to that prison inside his head.

Ahead of him Madison stopped. It would take him only a minute to bring her down, and he struggled with the idea of what to do with her when he did. Killing her would solve many of his problems, but he knew it would be impossible. Since the merger had begun, it was as if a switch had been flicked somewhere inside his head, preventing him from being able to do what he did best.

And even if he could still kill, he doubted that he would be able to hurt Madison. It was Tom again, injecting his stupid feelings into Tyler's head. It made him feel weak.

Tyler raced into the room just as the mechanical creature charged toward Madison. He slowed, mesmerized by the sight of this fascinating amalgam of biology and technology. He had learned about these biomechs during his training with the Janus Project, but he'd never dreamed he would see one in the flesh . . . *and metal*. Its body was covered in a lightweight metal

197

armor, its sensory organs replaced with the best technology available at the time.

They were to be the ultimate in disposable soldiers, common animals, mostly primates—apes—turned into killing machines by the latest in cybernetic technology. No morals, feelings, or grieving families to deal with, the biomechs were going to be a solution to modern warfare.

But that was before the pencil pushers realized what their new soldiers were going to cost. It took close to eight million dollars to outfit one ape with the technology and armament needed to turn it into a soldier. The thing must have ended up here on guard duty. Well, that explained the biscuits and the water trough.

The cybernetic animal stopped its charge, and Tyler could hear the faint whirring sounds of servomotors and optical enhancements as it sized up this new threat.

Then, deeming him more of a threat than Madison, it attacked with a bone-chilling cry.

The creature moved with incredible speed and fluidity, and Tyler couldn't help being impressed, but as the biomechanical animal charged, Tyler was moving as well, pulling the gun from his back pocket. He fired two shots in succession, aiming for the small unarmored sections on the animal's chest. He missed; the creature was faster than any human target he'd ever fired on. But the gunfire did force it to reassess its attack strategy, and it darted for cover behind some of the storage crates. Tyler tensed, listening carefully.

The ground in front of him erupted in machine-gun fire, and he jumped backward to see the mechanical ape running along the tops of the crates, an automatic weapon having emerged from a housing attached to its arm.

Diving for cover, Tyler took aim, fired four more shots, and actually managed to hit the machine gun, disabling it. The biomech stopped, studying its damaged weaponry, and Tyler fired again at its face, using the last of the bullets in his gun. The animal squealed as the lenses that had replaced its eyes exploded in a shower of sparks and colored glass.

The creature tumbled from its perch, clattering to the ground. Tyler crossed the warehouse. He stood above the beast, removing the empty clip and preparing to insert another. He couldn't help but feel a strange connection with the animal—created to be weapon and then locked away, just waiting for the day it would be called to action. He snapped the new clip into his gun and chambered a round. He took aim at the pathetic creature, preparing to put a bullet into its brain.

The biomech suddenly leapt up, its metal-sheathed teeth sinking into the flesh of his wrist. Tyler screamed, the gun dropping from his hand. He reacted instinctively—very much like an animal himself, digging the fingers of his other hand into the damaged mechanics surrounding the ape's eye. Howling in pain, Tyler dug deep.

The biomech let go with a wail just as soon as Tyler's fingers touched something moist—something all too fragile. He jumped back, clutching his injured arm to his chest. It was painful to move his hand, but at least it was still relatively operational.

The animal was already on the move, its head moving oddly, searching for its enemy. The warehouse space had become deathly quiet except for the sound of nervous gasping breaths coming from the other end of the room. Tyler turned to look at a wide-eyed and terrified Madison just as the biomech did. It zeroed in on the sound, tensing metal-sheathed musculature to attack.

It would have been the answer to his current dilemma, a way to eliminate a problem that he couldn't. But the messy emotions were screwing with his thought process again, and he started to stamp his feet and yell at the top of his lungs just as the killing machine was preparing to pounce.

The ape stopped mid-movement, swinging its head in the direction of the noise. Instinctively it raised its damaged arm weapon, wanting to strafe the area with gunfire, but was unable to. This seemed to frustrate the beast to no end. It tossed back its malformed head and roared.

Just before it charged.

Though damaged, it was still incredibly fast, slashing at him with razor-sharp fingers. Tyler grunted with exertion, rolling across the floor to escape the enraged beast.

The biomech stood perfectly still, listening. Slowly it raised its clawed hand to its face, sniffing at the blood that covered it. Tyler glanced down at his chest to see four gashes across the front of his shirt, dark stains seeping up from beneath.

He searched the room for anything he could defend himself with. Pretty ironic, to be in a room loaded with dangerous, high-tech weaponry and unable to gain access to any of it. He looked through the doorway, back toward where he had entered, and the germ of an idea began to take shape. It was risky, but at the moment it was the best he could come up with.

The biomech attacked again, fangs bared, razor claws ready to rend. Tyler fell backward to the floor, the mechanical animal passing over to land behind him. As Tyler scrambled to his feet, the biomech barked aggressively, striking at the ground in frustration, then spun around, preparing to charge again.

Tyler darted toward the doorway at top speed. He was running through the vehicle storage room, the sound of metal claws clattering across the concrete floor dangerously close behind him, when he suddenly changed course and headed toward the futuristic tank in the room's corner. He leapt atop the war machine and sprang at the submarine hanging from the ceiling above it, grabbing hold of its chains with his good hand.

Looking down from where he dangled on the swaying submarine, Tyler saw that the biomech had lunged, sinking its metal teeth into the front armament of the tank. The animal recoiled, growling angrily. Tyler kicked off one of his sneakers and sent it across the room, where it landed with a thud. The biomech responded to the sound, bounding from atop the tank to investigate.

Tyler angled his body, increasing the swing of the submarine, and let go at the precise moment he needed to, sailing through the air and coming down in a roll in front of the short hallway. He kicked off his other sneaker and ran in his stocking feet down the incline to the security door.

The sound of metal claws clattering on concrete grew louder as he pressed the combination into the numbered keypad. The door started to open, the red light flashing. Tyler slipped through and raced toward the virus storage chamber. He punched the number code into that door as well and heard a snakelike hiss as the room was unsealed.

Tyler entered, the blast of cold air invigorating on his sweat-dampened flesh. He grabbed a fire extinguisher from the wall, wedging it in the doorway, preventing the hermetically sealed door from closing behind him. An alarm bell began to sound as he ducked between the rows, his eyes searching for something he had seen earlier—something that could help him stop this seemingly unbeatable enemy.

Tyler had read about it during his training on alternate forms of warfare.

In its normal state—if one could call it that—the disease was called necrotizing fasciitis. It was a nasty bacteria that attacked fatty tissue and muscle, rotting it away, completely treatable with the right antibiotics when caught in time.

But that had been before a biological research team started to play with it, mutating it into something far more dangerous. In fact, that same team had literally been consumed in minutes when the voracious superbug was accidentally released in the lab. All that had remained were bloody bones.

Tyler held the canister of flesh-eating bacteria

carefully in his hand for a moment. He imagined he could feel the hungry organisms moving inside—eager to escape, to consume. Then the sounds of the approaching killer interrupted his thoughts and he wedged the canister into the waistline of his jeans and scaled the side of one of the storage racks.

It wasn't long before the biomech came around the corner, its metal-sheathed neck extended as it sniffed the cold air, searching for his scent. The technologically enhanced animal stiffened, lowering its head to the spot where he had been standing.

Tyler screamed, pulling the canister of death from the waistline of his pants as he dropped. He landed on the biomech's back and held on, wedging his good arm—his strongest arm—beneath the animal's reinforced throat. It howled, throwing its body up against the heavy racks, trying to dislodge him, but he held fast.

The biomech thrashed, its actions becoming more frantic as its frustration raged. The beast hurled itself to the floor. Explosions of color suddenly erupted before Tyler's eyes as the oxygen exploded from his lungs. He wasn't sure how much more punishment his body could take and decided that it was time to act. This was kill or be killed, and while Tom's presence inside him was holding Tyler back from certain actions, the drive for self-preservation at least was something the two of them shared.

Still holding fast to the hard, armored body, Tyler brought his other arm, the one holding the canister, around to the front of the beast's face. He could feel it stiffen as it sensed an opportunity to sink its metal teeth into its prey. Tyler teased it a bit more, bringing the hand holding the container closer and then pulling it away. The creature bit blindly at the air, its metal jaws snapping like a bear trap. And finally Tyler brought the canister within its reach.

The biomech bit down on the metal object, releasing the dangerous contents in an explosion of hissing coolant as the seals on the canister were broken.

Tyler was already diving across the room, holding his breath, imagining the flesh-eating bacteria slowly awakening, becoming active, and attacking their closest source of sustenance.

The creature roared behind him, a stranger sound than he had heard before from the animal, and he suspected that his plan had worked. Now all he had to do was contain the beast and everything would be—

The blow from behind sent him hurtling into a nearby wall. Tyler fought to stay conscious, flipping onto his back to see the mechanical ape dragging itself across the floor toward him, leaving a dark, moist trail in its wake. Blood oozed from its armored plating as the bacteria began to dissolve its flesh. He scrambled away from the animal, not wanting any contact with its newly infected blood, but the blow had addled his brain.

He was dizzy, unable to recover enough speed to avoid contact with the enraged animal. It crawled toward him quickly, a thick viscous blood mixed with mucus leaking from its open mouth as the flesh of its internal workings began to liquefy.

Tyler had pulled back his foot, ready to kick the beast square in the face as it tried to crawl on him, when the sound of a single gunshot suddenly filled the air. He watched as part of the biomech's face dissolved into pieces of broken metal, rotting skin, and bone. The creature squealed with a mixture of rage and pain as it continued to die, flipping onto its back, its body jerking in spasms as it fought to stay alive.

Tyler flipped onto his belly and looked up at the most unexpected of sights. Madison Fitzgerald stood there, pistol in hand. He wasn't sure if she had ever fired a weapon before: judging by the vacant expression on her face, he doubted it. It had been a relatively good shot, he thought as she helped him to stand. Perhaps with some proper training, there was room for her in the business of covert operations and assassination.

She helped him from the room, and he paused

momentarily to kick the fire extinguisher away, allowing the door to seal behind them. "We don't want anything in there getting out," he said, finding that he needed to lean on her.

They moved farther out into the hallway outside the storage room, watching through the large glass window as the biomech succumbed to the virulent necrotizing fasciitis. The flesh and muscle beneath the armored exterior were melting like candle wax, a thick puddle of gore spreading beneath the thrashing beast as it continued to die. It seemed to look at them momentarily, its head lolling on its weakening neck, and Tyler felt an uncommon pang of sympathy for the experimental instrument of war.

He took a deep breath. He was feeling better now, able to stand on his own again, the pain in his arm and his back not so bad.

"Thanks," he said turning to Madison with a smile, reaching out to take the gun that she was still holding. It was time to get back to business.

"Now, where did you put my canister?"

Tom wasn't sure how long he had been falling, only that it seemed like a very long time. At some point he thought he'd lost consciousness and dreamed that he was being chased by a freaky mechanical ape.

He was actually happy when he hit ground, the sudden impact shocking him back to an awakened state—or at least as much as a person could be considered awake when trapped inside their own psyche. The darkness was firm beneath him, and he was completely blind—not an ounce of light to be found. Maneuvering into a sitting position, Tom sat in the inky black and contemplated what he should do next.

And then he felt that pull again. Careful to maintain his balance, he stood and slowly turned his body around, searching for the source of his attraction. It was like wading into the flow of a stream, and he let himself be drawn forward, breathing a sigh of relief each time his footfalls actually landed on solid surface.

Tom continued, his steps growing more assured, the tug on his person becoming stronger. And as he walked, he had to wonder how deep inside his own mind he had gone. And what his purpose was for being here was—what it was exactly that had drawn him through the fortified metal door to this place of complete darkness, beyond the hallway of memories.

And then, off in the distance, he saw a soft glow. It reminded him of the fireflies he had seen in his backyard sometimes during the summer months. But the closer he got, the larger the area of luminescence became. It was a beacon of light in the shadow, and as he grew near, he realized that something was inside the illuminated circle, and it was calling to him.

It wasn't a voice exactly but a feeling, a sense that the circle was where he needed to be now, that getting to it was something he was supposed to be doing. He remembered the last time he had felt that way, when he'd accepted the idea of merging with Tyler Garrett, allowing some of the assassin personality's character traits to become part of his own. It had felt right, as if he were correcting something that was inherently wrong.

The current drawing him toward the circle of light was even stronger now, and he ran, practically carried by the force of it. And finally he saw what was in the middle of the light, but he was more confused than ever before.

It was a bed, a tiny bed. And in the center of the bed, curled up into a tight little ball, was a sleeping child.

A little boy, no more than six.

For the briefest of moments Tom was afraid, stopping short, even though the force continued to tug at him, eager for him to come closer. What was it about the little boy, fast asleep, that terrified him so much? He kept his distance, continuing to stare.

The child stirred, a spastic jerk of his leg, and kicked off the covers. He was wearing pajamas that resembled hospital scrubs. Succumbing to the force of the pull, Tom found himself moving closer.

The fear was still there but manageable as he gazed down from the foot of the little bed at the sleeping boy. Tom resisted the urge to cover the exposed child back up again with the blanket.

Who are you? Tom wondered, staring down at him. *And why are you in this dark place inside my mind?*

As if answering his question, the child languidly rolled over on the bed, and Tom suddenly knew the answer.

It's me. This child is me.

•   •   •

Even though she had saved his life, Tyler Garrett was getting a little tired of Madison Fitzgerald and her foolishness.

"I'm gonna ask you again," he said, applying a certain amount of pressure to his grip on her upper arm to show he meant business. "Where did you put my canister?"

She started to wince in pain but then fought it back, looking defiantly into his eyes. "I don't know. In all the excitement I must have dropped it."

He fought back the urge to strike her, certain that it wouldn't do him a bit of good—though it might have provided him with the littlest bit of raw satisfaction.

But then he noticed the way she was standing; there was a certain stiffness to her posture that he hadn't noticed before.

"Damn, girl," he said, smiling at her display of courage. Tyler lunged at her, and she threw herself back against the corridor wall.

"Careful," he cooed, reaching behind her and down into the back of her low-cut jeans. "Wouldn't want to have an accident."

He pulled the small canister from the back of her pants, pushing her away as she tried to fight him for it. "You almost had me convinced that you'd hidden it," he said, admiring his prize, relieved that it was back in his possession.

"I would have," she spat, "if I hadn't been so concerned about saving your stupid life."

Tyler turned away from her, walking back toward the storage area. "Thanks for that, by the way," he said. His wrist was throbbing painfully where the biomech had squeezed it, and there were spots on his body that felt like they'd been put there by a blowtorch, but it was nothing that he wouldn't survive. Tyler actually relished the pain; it proved that he was alive—that he was real.

"I should have let that thing kill you," Madison said.

He turned his head slightly to look at her, seeing that she was fighting back the tears as she followed.

"But then Tom would be dead too," she said, lowering her gaze. "And I couldn't stand the thought of that."

Tyler resisted the insane urge to go to her—certain that any attempt he made to make her feel better would have been met by her trying to tear out his throat or something equally nasty.

She didn't care about him and never would. It was Tommy she wanted, and he was just going to have to get used to that.

He couldn't wait to finish this mission and have Kavanagh get rid of Tom and his pain-in-the-ass emotions for good.

Halfway across the weapons storage area Tyler knew that something was wrong. He tensed as he walked, not letting his concern show. There was electricity in the air, and he had to wonder if more biomechs were about. But then the soldiers emerged from their hiding places, multiple beams of red laser light pinpointing his vital organs as they aimed their guns at him.

"Freeze, Garrett," a familiar voice barked, and he did as he was told.

Pandora agent Abernathy stood beside Director Tremain and, beside him, his old handler Victoria Lovett.

Tyler smiled. "Did we switch sides, Mom?" he asked the woman while counting the number of soldiers.

There were ten that he could see, maybe more that he couldn't. From out of the corner of his eye he watched as one of them escorted Madison past him, bringing her to safety.

"Lower the canister to the floor, gently," Tremain ordered.

Tyler glared at the older man. "You didn't say the magic word," he said with a grin.

The director wasn't amused, and the laser sights were still aimed at Tyler's head and heart. If he was going to make a move, he would have to do it now. He started to bend his knees, bringing the canister down to the floor. He dropped it, pretending to slowly rise, and then the muscles in his legs coiled like steel springs as he bolted, propelling himself toward the first soldier, about four feet away.

Beams of red laser light swirled around like fireflies as they tried to get a bead on him.

Two feet from his target Tyler extended his arms, ready to snatch the weapon away from the man.

And that was when he felt it—felt *him*.

He'd been wondering where his other half was, hoping that some miracle had happened and that Tom had somehow been absorbed by his brain. No muss, no fuss; gone just like that.

Attempting to ignore the presence in his mind, Tyler grabbed the gun and pulled it toward him, dragging the soldier with it. He wanted the gun, not the man attached by the strap across his shoulder.

It's time, Tom Lovett said, and it was as if he were standing right beside him, whispering in his ear. This couldn't have happened at a worse moment.

Tyler threw an elbow into the soldier's throat, collapsing his windpipe, yanking the gun away from his choking body and breaking the shoulder strap. He was ready to rock. He had spun toward his enemies, finger tensed on the trigger, ready to fire, when the annoying voice inside his head spoke again.

Lights out, it said, and he could feel it coming. Like a runaway freight train it was upon him: a full-fledged narcoleptic attack.

And he could do nothing as he felt the darkness begin to claim him, locking eyes with Christian Tremain, trying so hard to fire his weapon—to take some of his enemies down with him as he went.

"Take him," Tremain said, his words slurred in slow motion.

And the weapons trained on him opened fire, but he didn't feel a thing.

He was already fast asleep.

Brandon Kavanagh strolled into the control center, poured himself a steaming cup of coffee, took a seat in front of the multiple television screens—all tuned to myriad twenty-four-hour news stations—and started his wait for the first signs that the apocalypse had come.

Well, at least a good outbreak of plague, anyway.

Noah Wells was already in the room, barely acknowledging his presence as he entered.

"Anything yet?" Kavanagh didn't even know why he asked the question. The rough timetable that had been set up with Garrett still had at least twelve hours remaining before the virus was to be released, but who knew, he might have been early.

"A hurricane by the name of Margaret is going to hit the Bahamas, the president is forming a research team to further investigate the effects of global climate change, the economy is in the crapper, and we're still fighting the war on terror," Wells answered, never missing a beat. "But nothing about a killer plague wiping out a small town in the Midwest, sorry."

Kavanagh took a sip from his coffee. "Sucks about the economy," he said.

Wells nodded. "Probably be a tough holiday season for retailers."

"Ouch," Kavanagh responded. "Didn't even think of that."

"What's the name of the town again?" Wells asked. He got up from his seat, going to the coffee machine to refill his cup.

"Plainville," Kavanagh said. "Population two thousand, six hundred and nineteen."

There was a story on one of the monitors about a squirrel that could water-ski. That was some hard-hitting news.

If only they knew what was coming.

"Why Plainville?" Wells asked.

Kavanagh turned to look at his head of security.

"I'm just curious. I'm sure there are other little Midwest towns that could've fit the bill. . . . Why Plainville?"

"No reason," Kavanagh answered with a slight shake of his head. "It just fit the criteria: small town, probably has a parade on the Fourth of July that the whole town turns out for, a real slice of good old US of A. And won't it be something terrible when they all turn up dead."

"Just awful," Wells agreed, strolling back to his chair.

"But it'll be just the thing to make our potential foreign investors sit up and take notice," Kavanagh said with a slow nod. "When they see the kind of damage our product was responsible for, they'll be shoveling money into our secret Swiss bank accounts."

Wells frowned.

"What's wrong?" Kavanagh asked.

"It just kind of sucks that it had to get this nasty, y'know?" the man commented. "But I guess when push comes to shove . . ."

Kavanagh felt bad, he really did, but they had forced his hand. All he wanted was to sell the technology that he'd developed, to live off the hard work that he had devoted a large portion of his life to. Was that so wrong of him?

But then Pandora had to get involved, scaring away his customers, and suddenly he found himself backed into a corner, being forced to prove what he was capable of.

They'd left him no choice.

Grandma would've been proud.

Brandon was amazed at how easy it had been.

Trudging through the woods, returning to his home victorious, his grandmother's words echoed in his mind. He'd taken control of his fear and used it to make his problem go away.

It was a known fact that Tyler Garrett got up real early in the morning and went fishing at Kole's Creek and a known fact that if you wanted to go fishing, you didn't go there.

Sunup had been at least an hour away as Brandon had carefully made his way through the thick brush, the slowly lightening sky helping him to see. There was a part of him—an old part, a part that didn't listen to his grandma—that hoped that the bully wasn't there, that he'd decided not to go fishing that morning and stayed in bed. And for a moment that older part that was still afraid of his grandmother, that thought she smelled the way a dead body just might smell—that part of him thought that its wishes were answered.

From a small hill he'd looked down through an overgrown thicket and tangled brush at Kole's Creek and found it peacefully empty. The moon and the stars were reflected in the natural blackness of the creek, its surface smooth as glass, and at that very moment Brandon Kavanagh thought that it was the most beautiful sight he'd ever seen.

Everything was different at that moment, his grandma's hissing words silenced in his head. There was only himself, the creek, the forest, and the dwindling night. He wished that he could always feel this way.

But wishes were for magic lamps and falling stars, and he hadn't come across any of them since leaving his grandmother's home in the early hours of the morning.

Tyler Garrett arrived not two seconds after Brandon wished he wouldn't, the serene setting suddenly disturbed by the bully's hacking and coughing as he emerged from the woods, fishing pole slung over his shoulder.

Brandon sighed then, knowing that after this point, everything was going to be different. Clutching the cane his grandfather had made, he left his observation place to go down to the creek. The cane seemed to give him a strange surge of power; it was as if the moment his grandmother had put it in his hands, the way things were supposed to be—had to be—suddenly became clear, the old walking stick acting as a kind of focus.

Brandon moved carefully, silently through the forest, traveling around the creek, wanting to approach Garrett from behind.

He'd taken the cane while his grandmother was having her nightly bath, sneaking into her bedroom and snatching *it from where she'd left it hung around one of the posts of her bed. She wouldn't be needing the stick, and he'd planned to have it back to her long before she got up in the morning. It was sort of funny, the idea that had taken shape inside his head as to what to do about his problem hadn't become quite clear until the cane was in his possession.*

He'd thought about the different ways he could do this: calling to the boy from the woods, drawing him in, but it didn't feel right. Brandon's fear was great, and he needed to take control of it completely or he was sure it would kill him. Clutching the cane tightly in his hands, he emerged from his cover. Brandon expected the boy to turn immediately around, seeing him—freezing him in his beady-eyed stare—but it was almost as if his surroundings were somehow in league with him, stifling the sound of his approach, allowing him to creep up on Tyler Garrett completely unheard.

Staring at the back of the boy's shaggy head, Brandon remembered all the pain, hate, and rage that had been heaped upon him since Tyler had decided that it was his personal mission to make his life a living hell. He felt the punches again, the kicks, the words of scorn as they burrowed into his ears, taking root inside his brain. And he felt them all at once.

Well, what are you gonna do with it? *he heard his*

grandmother ask him, the cane—his hate and fear taken shape—clutched tightly in his hands. And he knew exactly what he wanted to do, what he needed to do, but decided that it couldn't be this way.

He couldn't come at his foe from behind; Tyler needed to know. He needed to know who it was that had taken his power—taken away his control. "Tyler," he said softly, the word leaving his mouth on a gentle puff of air.

And the boy turned, his big dumb face slack, his eyes dull, but then there was the spark of recognition, and with that, a glint of maliciousness was ignited. He looked like he was going to speak, to say something nasty.

But not this morning, Brandon thought, stepping toward the boy, the cane clutched tightly in both hands. And he reared back, swinging with all his might, the knotted end of the cane connecting with the side of Tyler's face, and he watched the lights go out as Tyler tumbled to the creek bank with a grunt.

Brandon was amazed at how easy it was.

He raised the cane above his head, bringing it down again on his unconscious foe's skull. The sight of blood glistening on his enemy's face, on the grip of the cane, froze him momentarily, shocking him into the realization of what he had just done—what he was about to do.

Are you ready for this? asked a voice in his head.

Yes, he told it, not wanting to be afraid anymore, and

he raised the weapon above his head, bringing it down again and again, smashing his fear, defeating it—driving it into the dirt.

Just like that it was done, and he knew that he was forever changed, that things for him would be different, and that if he ever felt fear again in his life, he would remember this moment and know what he was capable of.

The image of Tyler dead, beaten to death on the bank of Kole's Creek, stayed with him his entire walk back to the house, a constant companion filling him with a kind of strength and confidence he had never known. The house was silent as he entered through the back way, still far too early for any of the help to have arrived yet. The cane felt like it had become part of him, still firmly clutched in his hands, but he knew that he needed it to get it back to his grandmother before she awakened. And using his newfound strength—this courage—he'd climbed the stairs and, as silently as he could manage, opened the door and gone into the old woman's room.

His plan was to leave the cane beside her wheelchair, sneaking out of the room as quickly and silently as he had entered. But that wasn't how it worked out.

The light by his grandmother's bedside clicked on, freezing him in place.

Grandma stared at him standing there, her property in his hands, and he prepared himself for the worst. And the strange thing—the most wonderful thing—was that he wasn't afraid.

She squirmed herself up into a sitting position, pillows wedged behind her scrawny back. Her eyes never left him.

"Just look at you," she said, a bony arm coming out from beneath the covers to gesture at him. "Don't you look a fright."

And in the light he looked at himself, realizing that the front of his clothes—his shirt and pants—were spattered with dark red stains.

"Is that my cane you got there?" she asked him.

He held it out to her, and as he did, he saw that it too was covered in blood.

She waved him away, gesturing toward her bathroom across the room. "Get me a washcloth," she commanded.

He did as he was told, going into the bathroom and retrieving a used washcloth from the side of the bathtub. He passed a mirror that hung over the sink and saw that his face was spattered with red blotches, making him look like he had the chicken pox again.

He returned with the damp cloth.

"Now give them to me," she instructed. He handed both the cane and the cloth to her and stepped back as she started to wipe the cane clean.

"This ain't the only thing that needs a good wipin' down," she said, giving him a look.

He promptly turned to go.

"And after you're done cleanin' up, I want you to bring me those filthy clothes," she told him.

Nodding, he opened the door, and just as he was about to leave, she called to him again.

"How did it feel?" she said.

"Ma'am?" he questioned, coming back into the room, not sure if he had heard her right.

"I asked you how it felt."

"It felt . . . good," he told her, not sure if that was the correct way to describe it.

She chuckled, continuing to rub down the polished piece of wood, removing any stain that might have clung to it.

"You're a Kavanagh, all right," she told him, shaking her head with a smile. "Your granddaddy would've been proud."

Tyler awakened standing before a wall of thorns.

"Dammit," he barked, looking out over the body of thick, constricting vines that surrounded the ancient house.

His house.

He had been pulled down into a narcoleptic seizure and knew exactly who was responsible.

"Are you in there, Tommy?" he yelled over the tangle of thick, thorny vines. "Don't know what games you're playing, but you might as well accept that you're gonna lose. I'm in control now, big guy—I'm the dominant one now, and there ain't nothing you can do to change that."

Tyler stood before the vines, waiting for some kind of response from inside the house. The old structure remained silent; the only sound present was the moaning of the wind. He liked the sound, finding it strangely comforting. It had often been his only companion in the times that he'd waited to be activated.

"So it's gonna be like that," he muttered, stepping back from the heavy constriction of vines and concentrating with all his might on a particular area. Tyler's grin grew twice its size as the vines responded, twisting and writhing as their trunk-like bodies reconfigured themselves, forming a path through their mass leading directly to the front steps of the house.

"This is my place," he shouted, striding down the passageway. "I'm in control here—I'll always be in control here."

The pain was sharp, burning, and Tyler looked down to see that he had walked a little too close to one of the thorns and it had torn his shirt and the flesh beneath.

"I'll always be in control here," he said, this time more forcefully.

Just in case someone was listening.

Tom and the child walked hand in hand through the darkness.

The bed in which the little boy had been sleeping was far behind them now, a barely visible light far off in the distance.

The child's hand felt odd in his, the connection of his flesh to the boy's completing some kind of bizarre circuit. Tom's skin had started to itch as well, from the moment he'd understood who this child was. He glanced down and saw patches of rough discolorations on his arms and wrists.

Of course . . . it made perfect sense.

As they walked together, Tom's mind became filled with strange images, memories bubbling up through layers of mental flooring—flooding the house of his mind.

The remembrances were fragmented, staccato images from a brain not yet fully developed—a brain not yet capable of grasping the horrors of what was being done to it.

He remembered doctors—countless faces, both men and women, young and old—as they pricked and prodded. There were other children too, quite a few at first, and he wasn't so afraid until they started to go away. Every day there seemed to be fewer and fewer of them—comforting faces not there anymore.

Tom looked down at the child as they continued their stroll through the darkness. The little boy yawned, rubbing his tired eyes with his free hand as they trudged along. Gazing at the child, Tom could not help but realize that this sleepy-eyed little boy was the real Tom Lovett.

The flow of memories surged again, and Tom suddenly remembered the excitement and fear of flying in a plane—a little girl sitting in the seat beside him crying because she was afraid. He'd held her hand, trying to assure her that there was no reason to be scared even though he was terrified too.

Tom experienced the child's terror as his own, fighting the urge to collapse in tears, to curl into a tight little ball and escape the horror.

From the airplane they were loaded onto a bus and driven to a place—a big old house, a mansion.

The image of the sprawling home filled his mind, and Tom suddenly understood the origins of Tyler's mental construct. It was where the children had been taken—the original home of the Janus Project.

The memories that followed were an odd jumble of pain mixed with fear, people with lab coats holding clipboards and wearing fake smiles. But one man was nice. He had white hair and glasses and said that his name was Dr. Quentin. The nice doctor told them not be afraid. He assured them that he didn't want to hurt them.

And Tom believed him.

But the other doctors were different. They didn't care. They were scary, and they stuck needles into the kids—inside their heads—and strapped them down so that they couldn't move.

Tom suddenly began to gag, choking on the taste of rubber, experiencing the memory of a mouth guard being shoved into his mouth, keeping his teeth apart. Strapped on the bed, he could see other children like him—including the girl whose hand he'd held on the plane—restrained, and he wished that somebody would hold his hand then, because he was so very afraid.

Tom couldn't take it anymore, dropping to his knees in the place of darkness. He wished he could take the black that surrounded him and wrap it around himself like a blanket, escaping into the void. He didn't want to remember anymore—he didn't want to know the child's pain.

His pain.

He felt the soft touch of a hand on his shoulder and looked up into the child's face. There was strength in the little boy's eyes, something that would desperately be needed if they were to survive this ordeal.

Tom climbed shakily to his feet, and the child smiled, taking his hand.

The little boy was leading him now, deeper and deeper into the all-encompassing landscape of shadow. And off in the distance, so far away that it sounded like a whisper, they heard a voice.

An angry voice.

And they moved toward it.

• • •

The double doors to the decrepit mansion exploded open with the force of his kick, one of the hinges pulling from the ancient wood of the door frame, causing the door to hang awkwardly to one side.

"Where are you?" Tyler screamed.

He had every intention of killing Tom Lovett.

His shoulder began to throb and he glanced at the thorn wound, feeling just the slightest hint of panic. What had started off as a cut, two inches in length at most, had turned into something far worse. The wound was obviously infected, the skin around it an angry red, weeping a thick, viscous fluid. He tenderly touched it with his fingertips. He'd seen these effects when Tom Lovett had taken control and he—and all that defined him—was being absorbed.

Tyler studied the backs of his hands, noticing the blotchy redness slowly beginning to form there. It was happening again.

"No," he said, his fury growing. "No, I will not allow this."

He moved farther into the entryway, darting toward the sitting room. "Where are you, Tom Lovett!" he screeched. "Show yourself before I—"

"I'm right here," said a voice, interrupting his rant, and Tyler came to a sliding stop before going into the sitting room. He turned, standing in the archway to the grand old room, watching as Tom descended the staircase.

And he wasn't alone.

A child was with him; a child, barefoot and wearing light blue hospital scrubs. There was something about the little boy—something calming, peaceful.

Disturbingly familiar.

"*We're* here," Tom said, correcting himself.

"What's this?" Tyler asked with a mocking laugh. "Found yourself a friend, did ya?"

They stopped on the stairs, both of them staring at him as if he were some kind of freak.

"I found more than that," Tom replied.

Tyler slowly moved toward them, his thoughts already filling up with the hundreds of ways in which he could eliminate Lovett and the child if he had to.

"Who is he?" Tyler asked. "Long-lost childhood friend dug up from one of the pockets of memory we've got lying around in here? Somebody who once shared his juice box with you—or let you play with his dump trunk one day when you was feeling exceptionally vulnerable?"

"You know who he is," Lovett said, and suddenly a thought—a horrible, horrible thought—flowed into Tyler's mind, and yes, yes, he did know who the little sandy-haired boy was.

233

And at that precise moment he knew who had to die first.

Does Tyler understand what this means? Tom wondered, staring down at his more vicious half from the stairs. He certainly hoped so; things would go so much smoother if he'd just accept reality.

The child had seemed drawn to Garrett, navigating the darkness of their psyche, pulling him along with intense purpose. They had emerged from the shadows into the muted light of the endless hallway, Tyler's screams of rage summoning them to the foyer. For a moment he had been afraid, planting his feet as the child tugged on his hand.

And then the child had smiled at him, and without saying a word, Tom knew that this was the way it was supposed to be—how it had to be if things were ever going to be right again.

Before Tom could say a word, what he had foolishly mistaken for understanding suddenly shifted to burning rage. Tyler darted up the stairs at them, his fist pulled back to hit the child.

Tom jumped between them, blocking the punch aimed at the child's face.

"Out of the way, Tommy," Tyler hissed. "Don't make this any harder than it has to be."

Tyler lashed out at him, and Tom barely had time to deflect the blow. He punched back, clipping the side of his twin's face, but Tyler dodged him and his knuckles just grazed his cheekbone.

"Almost got me," Tyler growled, reaching out to grab him by the front of his shirt. "But *almost* can get you killed."

Tyler threw Tom over the side of the stairway. Tom landed in a crumpled heap in the entranceway below. He scrambled to his feet, shocked by Tyler's incredible strength.

Garrett glared at him from the stairs. "You stay right there," he ordered. "I'll be down to deal with you in a minute."

Tyler turned to face the child.

"Leave him alone!" Tom screamed, racing up the steps. When he reached the top, Tyler spun around, slapping him across the face so savagely he felt his jaw pop out of place as he sailed through the air. He landed in a heap back in the entranceway. The pain was incredible, firework explosions of color erupting in front of his eyes as he fought a growing nausea to get to his feet.

I have to do something, Tom thought feverishly, and he listened to the moans of the wind outside turning to screams in response to his inner turmoil, and he again remembered Tyler's words on his first visit to the mansion.

This is my place, Tommy, he'd told him. *It responds to my feelings.*

Through a pain-filled haze he saw that Garrett had one of his hands wrapped around the child's throat, choking him.

The wind outside roared like a wild animal trapped in a cage, and in his mind Tom saw it that way—like a thing alive—and suddenly the foyer was filled with a raging wind, a wind roused by Tom's own anger, a wind that was part of an environment that responded to *his* feelings as well.

It was as if a tornado had touched down in the mansion entryway, and shielding his eyes against the flying debris kicked up by the powerful winds, he watched as Tyler Garrett was yanked away from the boy, picked up by the maelstrom, taken from the stairs, and hurled into the far wall.

And as abruptly as it had started, the wind died down to a haunting moan. Tom knew that his time was limited, that the killer would quickly recover.

Lurching past the stairs, Tom checked on the child and found him sitting there, clutching the wood railing, a surprising look of calm on his face.

"Get out of here," Tom told him, gesturing with his

hand. "Go on and hide someplace before—"

"There's no place the little bastard can hide here where I couldn't find him," Tyler said, sailing across the room toward him.

The heel of his foot connected with Tom's face, sending him lurching backward.

The pain was kicked up another notch. Tom could almost hear the grinding of his broken ribs.

"I liked that trick with the wind, Tommy," Tyler said, touching the back of his head. His fingers came away red. "Nice to see you thinkin' on your feet."

He wasn't exactly sure how he did it, but Tom managed to stand, charging across the room at Tyler. Garrett knocked him back down with ease.

"You've lost, Tommy," he said. "The strongest one of us has won—get used to it."

Tom pushed himself up from the floor. "You're wrong," he grunted, managing to rise to a kneeling position.

"No," Tyler answered with a shake of his head. "I was always the real deal," he continued with a chilling smile. "It was you they tacked on, cobbled together from bits and pieces of different personalities."

Tyler darted forward, lashing out with his foot, kicking Tom on the side of the head and sending him sprawling back to the floor.

"You were just a mask to disguise a killer," he said.

And Tom started to laugh. Even though his head was spinning and his mouth was filled with the taste of blood, he couldn't stop himself. He just couldn't believe that his other half could be so stupid.

"Good to see that you didn't lose your sense of humor," Tyler said. "Wonder which one of the techs gave you that?"

"I don't believe you," Tom said, pushing himself up again into a sitting position. He looked at the killer—a twisted reflection of himself—and no longer felt fear or hate. He actually felt pity for Tyler Garrett. "You actually believe that pile of crap you're shoveling?"

He watched a look of confusion creep across Garrett's face. It was true; Tyler didn't understand at all.

Tyler pulled back his arm, ready to strike as Tom stared at him defiantly. "Go ahead, smash my face in," he shouted. "It won't change the fact of what we are—what we both are."

"I don't have any idea what you're talking about," Tyler screamed.

"Neither of us is real," Tom replied sadly. "We're both masks—artificial personalities grafted onto a pre-existing one—one that never got a chance to develop."

The expression on Garrett's face was one of shock

and horror. "It's not true," he spat, spinning around to see that the little boy was standing directly behind him. "It's not true!" he screamed at the child.

Tom got up from the floor, the pain in his side, on his face, having become a dull throb. "It is and you know it," he said, moving closer.

The child was looking up at him, a peaceful calm registering on his face. Tyler recoiled from the boy, jumping backward, afraid of what was coming next.

Tyler bumped into Tom, spinning around to look frantically into his eyes. "I'll . . . I'll kill you both," he said halfheartedly.

"No," Tom said. "We're way past that now."

Tyler looked away from him and to the child. Then he looked at his hands, at the dark, discolored blotches that were blossoming there. "I don't . . ." he began, turning to Tom again. "I don't want to die like this."

Tom remembered noticing the blotches of discoloration on his body when he'd first realized the truth of what the child represented. Yes, it was disturbing, but just a part of the process.

What did Dr. Quentin call it? he thought calmly. *Unification.*

He had no idea what the final outcome would be. As far as he knew, his personality could completely cease to exist, the assassin that he'd shared his mind with becoming completely dominant. It could happen, but it was a risk that needed to be taken. Tom couldn't live like this anymore.

"It's not about dying," he said, coming to stand beside the little boy. Tom reached down to take the child's hand in his. "It's about becoming whole."

The boy held out his other hand to Tyler Garrett.

A low rumble could be heard—felt—throughout the ancient mansion, the floor shaking beneath their feet. Huge jagged cracks like lightning bolts appeared on the walls; chunks of plaster dropped down from the ceiling to shatter on the floor.

It won't be long now before this place ceases to exist, Tom guessed as the house continued to crumble around them. *It won't be needed anymore.*

Tom watched as Tyler tentatively reached for the child's hand.

"I wonder if it'll hurt," the killer personality thought aloud, taking the boy's hand in his, seemingly resigned to his fate.

"Don't know," Tom said, reaching out with his own hand to Garrett to complete the circle. "We'll just have to take that chance."

The wind was screaming now, sections of the roof being torn away by destructive elemental forces to reveal a pitch-black void outside.

"Then what are we waitin' for?" Garrett asked with typical bravado, taking hold of Tom's hand. "Let's get this show on the road."

There was a searing flash as their hands entwined, a light so bright that it burnt all away.

Everything old was gone, leaving behind only the new.

One mind.

One body.

Unity.

CHAPTER 18

He hadn't returned to his quarters to go to bed, choosing instead to remain in front of the monitors.

Kavanagh stared at the multiple screens, eyes darting from one to another, searching desperately for some sign that his plan had been successful.

"How much longer are we going to wait?" Wells asked, standing in the doorway of the room, eyes red from lack of sleep.

Kavanagh gnawed at the skin at the edge of his thumb, pulling away a painful strip of flesh with his teeth, but the pain was nothing compared to what he was feeling at that moment.

The pain of failure, now, that was excruciating.

"What do you think went wrong?" Kavanagh asked.

Wells pushed off from the doorway, coming into the room. "Do you actually want me to answer, or are you just going to get all pissed off and tell me to shut my mouth when I give you my opinion?"

Kavanagh turned his head slowly to fix him with an icy glare. "I wouldn't have asked if I didn't want to know what you thought."

"I think he got caught," Wells answered. "Simple as that. I think he gave it his best, but sometimes your best just isn't enough."

"There was a lot riding on this," Kavanagh said. "We're going to look like fools to the community."

The community. It was like they were talking about an organization of local businessmen—Earl down at the five-and-dime or Big Bobby who owns the filling station across the street, Kavanagh mused. *Instead of a loose conglomerate of the world's most dangerous terror organizations.*

"I'd rather look like a fool than wind up back in Pandora custody," Wells said. "We've given it enough time. I think it would be wise to put our contingency plans into effect and get the hell out of Dodge. As far as we know, they could be on their way here now, and that's not good."

Kavanagh knew that his friend was right, that the longer they stayed in one place, the better their chances were of being caught, and he was damned if he was going to let that happen, but he couldn't get past the idea that he was running away for a second time.

Briefly he imagined being in custody at a Pandora facility, being questioned by Tremain. *Oh, you'd like that, wouldn't you,* Kavanagh thought, imagining a smug smile on the director's weathered features.

No, he couldn't stand for that, but to avoid it, he had to run.

A Kavanagh doesn't run, boy, he heard his grandmother croak from her big old bed.

"I've had just about enough of you," the man muttered aloud.

"This is what I mean," Wells suddenly said, exasperated. "You ask for my opinion, I give it, and then you toss it away like—"

"I wasn't talking to you," Kavanagh interrupted.

Wells went silent, knowing better than to ask who it was exactly he'd been speaking to. Wells was good like that.

"Have the explosives been placed?" Kavanagh asked.

"The day we got here," Wells responded faithfully.

Kavanagh nodded. The Janus Project was dead; he'd pretty much come to that sad conclusion the moment he suspected that Sleeper One had not completed his assignment. He would go elsewhere, review his options, and see what he could salvage from the years of research.

Janus was dead, but Brandon Kavanagh was more than alive.

He looked at his watch. "Give the evacuation order and prep the explosives for detonation," he said, getting up from his chair. "I'd like to be out of here and on my way to someplace where they serve those fruity drinks with the umbrellas within the next two hours."

Wells nodded. "I think I can swing that," he said, reaching for the small walkie-talkie on his belt.

Satisfied, Kavanagh had started for his office when he heard the sound of a distant alarm. He stopped short.

"What's that?" he asked with caution.

Wells clicked off his walkie-talkie and went to the television monitor control station. "It appears that we have company," the head of security said, switching from the news broadcasts to the cameras outside the base.

A jeep had stopped at one of many fences that surrounded the seemingly abandoned military base, and somebody was standing outside the vehicle.

"Tyler Garrett!" Kavanagh exclaimed.

"What's he doing *here*?" Wells muttered.

As if in response, Garrett reached under his blood-stained shirt, producing a silver canister, which he held up, showing it to the hidden camera.

Kavanagh's eyes widened; he knew full well what the youth had in his possession. "I want to know what he's been up to," he said. "Put together a team and bring him down here," Kavanagh added, unable to pull his gaze from the Janus Project's crowning achievement. "Perhaps things aren't as bad as they seem."

"Do you really think that's a good—"

"Bring him," Kavanagh barked, eyes fixed to the monitors. "I want to know what he's been up to."

Wells nodded begrudgingly, reaching for his walkie-talkie as he strode toward the exit.

"And Wells," Kavanagh called out. "Be extra careful with the canister. We wouldn't want what's inside getting out . . . at least until I say so."

Wells might have lost the ability to feel pain, but it did nothing to quell his sense of suspicion.

Something didn't feel right about this situation, and he instructed his team of four to be on their toes.

Disembarking from their jeep, assault rifles at the ready, they approached the gate where Sleeper One was still standing.

"'Bout time you showed up," the young man said. "I was just considerin' turning around and heading back to Pandora, see what they would trade me for this." He held up the canister of Kamchatka virus. "Think they might be interested?"

Wells sensed his men tense, aiming their automatic weapons.

Sleeper One smiled widely. "Just kiddin'," he said. "I knew you guys would be out here to get me eventually."

"How did you know to find us here?" Wells asked. "Our base of operation was never revealed to you."

The sleeper smiled slyly. "And that's where a little initiative comes in handy," he said. "Before bustin' out of Pandora, I took the liberty of using some of their tracking equipment and triangulated the general whereabouts of our boss man's cell signal, y'know, just in case. And I would have to say it came in pretty handy."

Wells didn't like this at all.

"You shouldn't have come here," he said. "Your instructions were to break into the Crypt, liberate the virus, and release the contents in the town of Plainville."

Sleeper One moved closer to the fence. "Yeah, but I ran into a few unexpected obstacles," he explained. "Not sure how they knew, but Pandora was riding my tail most of the time." He held out his arms, showing off the condition of his clothes. It looked like he'd seen some action—he was a mess, his pants and shirt spattered with blood. "As you can see, I barely got out of there alive. If I had tried to execute the Plainville objective, they would have easily been there to stop it."

Wells tilted his head, scrutinizing the young man on the other side of the fence. "And using a little more of that initiative you mentioned earlier—"

"You got that right," Sleeper One blurted.

"You decided to bring what you stole here."

"Better in the hands of my employer than the enemy is what I always say."

Wells motioned for one of his men to open the gate, and Garrett entered with a swagger.

Wells blocked his path. "Hand it over," he ordered, holding out his hand.

The sleeper planted his feet, bringing the hand holding the silver canister close to his side. "Can't do it," he said. "I may have had to deviate from my original orders a bit, but I promised myself that I'd deliver this little package directly to Kavanagh."

Wells's men raised their weapons again.

"What if I insist?" he asked.

"Then we just might have ourselves a situation," Garrett said coldly.

Wells eyed him for a moment, knowing what the teen was capable of. "All right," he said with a nod. "We'll let you hold on to it—for now."

"Much obliged," Garrett said as the soldiers escorted him to the jeep. "I knew we could work this out like gentlemen."

They rode back to the mess hall in complete silence.

"And here I was thinking you were taking me for a bite to eat," Garrett said, breaking that silence as they cut through the abandoned cafeteria on the way to the elevator that would bring them back down into the installation.

They all entered the elevator, and the door slowly slid shut with a mechanical hum before the cab shuddered and they began their descent.

"So what's the story with this place?" Garrett asked, speaking to no one in particular. "This where they kept them crashed UFOs, or is this one of the places that the world's elite were supposed to come when the bombs started to fall?"

Wells remained silent, as did his soldiers.

"I see how it is," Garrett said, looking up at the ceiling. "I'm not part of your little club, so you treat me like a piece of dirt."

Wells glared at the boy, resisting the urge to draw his pistol and put a bullet in his skull. He hated the personality they'd created for this sleeper assassin; that whole good ol' boy thing was like nails on a blackboard to him. He'd always wondered why Kavanagh had allowed the techs to go that route.

"Shut up," Wells ordered.

He felt his heart rate begin to quicken as Garrett smiled and then started to laugh.

"Did I say something amusing?" Wells asked, his finger twitching on the trigger of his automatic weapon.

"It's the accent, isn't it?" Garrett said suddenly, raising the silver canister to chest level. "If I can't stand the sound of it, I can just imagine what it sounds like to everyone else."

And without any explanation, he twisted the cover on the metal canister, releasing a billowing mist that filled the inside of the elevator in a choking cloud.

I should have shot him when I had the chance, was the last thought Noah Wells registered before dropping into unconsciousness.

The Dragonfly transport craft hovered over a section of the Mojave Desert, advanced stealth technology rendering it undetectable to Kavanagh's base of operations a little over three miles away.

The craft's vertical takeoff and landing systems, VTOL for short, kept it floating above the desert floor, suspended on columns of air created by the craft's four shielded rotors extending outward from the body of the vehicle.

Plans for the Dragonfly, as well as its highly advanced stealth technology, had been liberated from a Middle Eastern research facility that Pandora had suspected had ties with one or more terrorist organizations. Though the facility had been cleared of any wrongdoing, the plans for the VTOL transport were retained and the designs perfected by a Pandora development team.

It was expected that the Dragonfly would become part of the military's arsenal by 2010, but until then, the prototype was being utilized by the Pandora Group on any number of its covert desert operations.

Tremain ejected the clip from his Glock, checking the amount of ammunition he had for what could have been the tenth time. Seeing that it was still satisfactory, he slid the clip back into the gun.

"Did the number of bullets happen to change this time?" Victoria Lovett asked from her seat across from him.

"What?" he replied, annoyed that his thoughts had been disturbed.

"The bullets in your gun," she said, pointing. "Did they happen to change?"

He barely smiled. "A nervous habit," he told her, slipping the gun back into the shoulder holster beneath his arm.

"How about letting me have one?" she asked.

Agent Mayer's forehead creased with concern.

"You've been brought along on an advisory level," Tremain said. "There's no reason for you to be armed and—"

"I'm going in with your team," Victoria interrupted.

"No, you're not," Tremain corrected, starting to get up from his seat. "My trust can only be extended so far, Ms. Lovett."

She reached out, grabbing hold of his arm. Agent Mayer stood, but Tremain just shook his head.

"What about *my* trust, Mr. Tremain? The trust I had when I helped you to bring in my Tom," she said, her gaze boring into his. "And where is he now, sir?" she asked him. "Where is my son now?"

He gently removed her hand from his arm and looked over at Agent Abernathy, headphones over his ears, fiddling with a portable tracking system.

"He's in," Abernathy said, giving a thumbs-up.

"I must be allowed to help my son," Victoria Lovett said with complete conviction, drawing Tremain's attention back to her.

The intensity in her gaze is nearly overwhelming.

"Fine," Tremain said. Looking at Agent Mayer, he continued. "Bring her along, but under no circumstances is she to have a weapon."

Tom pressed the collapsible air filtration mask to his face, waiting for the elevator to finally arrive at its destination.

He'd helped himself to a pistol, an assault weapon, and multiple clips of ammunition.

253

Can never have too much of that.

Looking at the unconscious men lying on the floor of the elevator cab, he was glad that he'd decided to go with the gas. Originally there had been an argument about the rigged viral canister's effectiveness versus a straight physical assault. He, of course, had been arguing for the straight physical assault, Tremain and Abernathy for the latter.

If he actually managed to make it out of this situation alive, he'd have to pass the information on that they had been right. Tom smiled wistfully with the memory of his last conversation with Madison. She had made him promise—crossing his heart and hoping to die—that he would be safe and come back to her.

Tom had no choice but to comply; she wasn't about to turn him into a liar.

The elevator came to a stop. He flipped off the safety on the automatic weapon just in case and waited for the doors to part.

He'd come awake on a transport plane, feeling like he'd been electrocuted, which, in a way, he kind of had.

The weapons that the Pandora assault team had used on him—on Tyler—at the Crypt had been a new kind of Taser, a weapon capable of shocking his body into oblivion with multiple, fifty-thousand-volt hits of electricity. Not enough to kill, but plenty to take him down for the count.

What had happened after Tyler had been captured was a little vague, but he knew that it had something to do with the place—the mansion that his other half had built somewhere inside his head—and a little boy.

He remembered the little boy, but after that, things got sort of hazy.

All he knew was that Tyler Garrett was gone—*No, not gone.* He was definitely not gone. Tom could sense his presence in just about everything he did now, what he knew, the way he moved, his attitude toward life. No, Tyler Garrett had finally become a part of him—two distinctly different colors blended together to create an entirely new one.

Despite Sleeper One's return to roost, Brandon Kavanagh had come to the decision that he still needed to pull up stakes and relocate his operations elsewhere. The likelihood that Pandora was close to pinpointing his whereabouts was probably greater than he would like to imagine, and even though he could hear his dear old grandma's sage advice to never run from a fight, he was about to do just that.

What's the old adage? he thought. *It's better to run and live to fight another day? Or some such nonsense.*

The security team filed into the lobby of the facility, each taking up position in front of the elevator doors just in case.

He would relieve his agent of the Kamchatka virus and proceed with the plans already set in motion to leave the stronghold that had served as Janus's core base of operations for the last five years. This was where the true work had been done, the dirty stuff that Pandora didn't need to know about. It would be sort of sad to see what he'd worked so hard to build destroyed, but he cheered himself with thoughts of the days ahead. With the Kamchatka virus in his possession, he believed that a bright future in the lucrative field of biological weaponry could be waiting for him.

The doors to the elevator opened with a hydraulic hiss, a billowing white gas flowing out into the lobby of the main level. Kavanagh reacted instinctively, moving toward the doorway to begin his escape, but something slowed his progress, practically holding him in place.

Sleeper One emerged from the choking cloud, weapon firing. He was truly something to see, his movements so fast that Wells's handpicked security team could barely get a bead on him, the gunfire from their weapons riddling the surface of the concrete walls instead of delicate flesh, muscle, and bone. Every time they seemed to believe they had him in their sights, he was already on the move.

Kavanagh watched with rabid interest as his creation took down the elite security team with disabling gunfire but not, it seemed, with the intention of killing.

Something had happened to his bloodthirsty teenage assassin, he thought, observing the boy with growing fascination. He recalled the numerous training exercises that the Tyler Garrett personality had undergone to perfect his efficiency and how many of them had ended in slaughter. This wasn't like him, not like him at all.

One of the team didn't have the good common sense to lie down and accept defeat. Struggling to his feet after being shot in the shoulder and leg, the mercenary drew his knife and attempted to dispatch his young attacker.

Kavanagh knew that he should have been gone at this point, retreating to his office to retrieve the last of his private and professional effects, but he stood transfixed.

The solider lunged with his blade, Sleeper One responding almost in unison. He avoided the attack with ease, darting forward to take hold of the soldier's arm, and broke it with one quick jerk. As the knife dropped harmlessly to the ground, the sleeper sprang back, spinning his body around and delivering a sidekick to the man's face, putting him down for the count.

Completing his spin, the sleeper planted both feet, body tensed, ready to meet the next wave of attack. But there was none to be had: the security squad was either unconscious or moaning fitfully on the floor of the installation's lobby.

And then the sleeper's eyes found him.

Kavanagh's first instinct was to run, but after witnessing what he just had, he determined that running would be pretty much pointless.

The sleeper pounced, springing across the expanse of lobby toward him, a look suddenly burning in his eyes that Kavanagh had, just mere moments ago, come to believe had somehow been extinguished.

But there it was, raging behind the face of a boy—the killer he'd worked so hard to create.

Tom took down the last of the soldiers waiting outside the elevator, then stood, waiting to see where the next attack would come from.

His eyes scanned the area in front of him, landing on a single figure standing across the room. Tom had never seen this man before in his life but at the same time knew exactly who he was.

Brandon Kavanagh.

And that was all that was needed to trigger the savagely visceral reaction he had on seeing the man. Tom wanted to kill him. He wanted to wrap his hands around his neck and strangle the life from him, and when that was done, he wanted to get a knife and cut his heart out, and when that was finished, he would take a gun and empty the bullets into the body, and finally he would find some gasoline and matches and set fire to the corpse, burning the beaten and bloody remains of the man to ash.

And that reaction barely scratched the intensity of the fury he was feeling at that moment.

Tom was seeing only red, bounding across the room with murder his intent, and the man stood his ground, never blinking, reaching into his pocket and withdrawing—not a weapon, but what looked to be a phone.

What's wrong with this picture?

Pulling back his fist, Tom prepared to strike.

Just as Kavanagh brought the phone up to his mouth and spoke.

"Activate."

He stopped before the man, feeling something wriggling around within the folds of his brain.

Kavanagh didn't move, watching him carefully.

Tom could feel something—*The microchip implanted in my brain,* he guessed—attempting to perform the function for which it was intended, to trigger a narcoleptic attack via satellite from wherever Kavanagh's ally on the other end of that phone was located. But it couldn't trigger what didn't exist anymore.

He slowly raised his head, the hint of a mischievous grin tugging at the corners of his mouth. The expression on Kavanagh's face was priceless, the cruel son of a bitch suddenly realizing that things weren't going to go as planned.

Tom reached for him, grabbing him by the front of his shirt and ripping the cell phone from his hand.

"It doesn't work like that anymore," Tom said into the tiny phone, and then smashed it to the floor. He swung his fist into the older man's face and sent him stumbling backward into the wall.

The man knew he was in trouble, scrambling to get to his feet, but Tom was already at him, wrapping his hands around his throat, pulling him up, and slamming him roughly back against the wall.

"I'm here to thank you for all you've done for me," Tom hissed, starting to squeeze.

"Don't mention it," Kavanagh wheezed through gritted, bloodstained teeth, and Tom noticed the man's eyes dart to an area just to the right behind him.

He started to turn just as a bullet clipped the top of his shoulder, throwing him forward. Kavanagh scrambled out from beneath him, throat bright red from where Tom had gripped it.

"I was beginning to wonder what I pay you for, Mr. Wells," Kavanagh said to the man stumbling from the elevators, pistol in hand.

Tom pushed himself up the wall, painfully aware of the red smear that he left on the painted cinder block as he rose. This was far from over.

"You mean it wasn't my talent for stimulating conversation?"

Kavanagh seemed annoyed by the man's wiseass response. "Just kill him and be done with it," he ordered, turning to quickly leave the room.

"From God's lips to my ears," the man said without a moment's hesitation, raising the pistol and firing repeatedly in Tom's direction.

Tom was already moving, pulling his own weapon from the waistline of his pants and returning fire.

The entryway filled with the sound of thunder.

Bullets were flying everywhere, but targets weren't being hit. Wells had taken cover by a stack of crates and Tom behind a heavy metal reception desk pushed over into a corner, its gray surface covered in a thick layer of dust.

There was an impatience in him now, something coiled tightly in the pit of his belly, something that cried to be unleashed, to express what it was capable of. A gun battle like this, where opponents were evenly matched, depending on the amounts of ammunition available, could go on for days.

And time was something he didn't have the luxury of—or the patience for.

Slipping a fresh clip of bullets into his gun, he emerged from his hiding place, bringing the fight directly to his enemy.

Wells jumped out from behind the crates and proceeded to fire.

Tom charged his enemy, firing shots from his own gun as he made his way closer to his target. This was what he preferred, a more direct approach to combat—more hands-on.

It was almost as if Wells understood what he was up to and was more than happy to oblige. The lanky man emerged from the shadows. He was fast and immediately relieved him of his gun, which was perfectly fine by Tom; the time for guns was over.

Tom threw a punch toward the man's face, connecting with the bridge of his nose with a loud snap. Blood gushed from the man's nostrils in a crimson spray.

"Good one," Wells said, and without pause he brought his knee up to chest level, snapping out with his leg, the heel of his military boot connecting with Tom's face. Tom flew backward, the power behind the kick making him see stars.

His opponent was on him in an instant, and Tom quickly recovered to meet this next attack. Wells threw a succession of punches, driving Tom backward as he evaded the lightning-fast strikes.

And all the while he was waiting for his moment. Waiting for the opportunity to end this as quickly and efficiently as possible. Wells launched a punch, exposing the soft patch of nerve clusters beneath his arm, and Tom reacted, darting beneath the blow, driving a balled fist into the extremely sensitive area, a blow that should have immobilized him.

It had no effect whatsoever.

Tom was surprised, and that turned into complete bewilderment as Wells locked his large hands around his throat and started to squeeze. Tom struggled to break the man's grip on his neck. He brought back both his hands, clapping them savagely against the sides of Wells's head, rupturing the man's eardrums, the trade-mark move of Tyler's that Tom had witnessed in flash-backs.

Amazingly, Wells's grip on Tom's throat only tight-ened even as thick dark blood began to ooze from Wells's ears. Spots of color blossomed before Tom's eyes as his need for oxygen became more immediate.

The man didn't appear to feel any pain, even when Tom brought his knee up into the guy's groin. Wells didn't so much as grunt, instead slamming Tom back-ward against a nearby wall.

He found his thoughts drifting, the explosions of color reminding him of Fourth of July fireworks. How easy it would be to stop fighting and accept his fate.

There are worse ways to die.

And that might have been how the old Tom Lovett

would have dealt with the situation—giving in—but that person didn't exist anymore and hadn't really in quite some time, since he'd heard the mysterious word *Janus* spoken in his dreams. When everything had changed.

Tom let his body go slack, and he felt Wells's hold on him loosen ever so slightly. Seizing the moment, Tom brought his arms up and then down with everything he had, finally managing to break the man's grip around his throat.

Tom filled his lungs with air and slid along the wall in an attempt to escape and regroup.

"Oh no, you don't," Wells growled, reaching out to take hold of his arm in a steely grip, pulling him back.

Tom rammed his knee up into the man's chest. There wasn't a doubt in his mind that some of the ribs had broken, but Wells looked totally unaffected.

Perplexed and a little frustrated, Tom put his newly acquired skills into overdrive, breaking free of the man's grip and launching a series of blows and kicks. Wells did what any trained combatant would do, blocking and following through with his own moves, but Tom was stunned by the way he shrugged off the severity of Tom's attacks. The man was bleeding from any number of places, but still he continued to fight, showing no sign of weakening.

Tom spun around, bringing his foot up in a snap

kick into the man's jaw. Wells fell back, blood leaking from his mouth.

But it did nothing to slow him down. The man charged at him with renewed vigor, the two slamming into the discarded reception desk. Wells was on top of him, his blood dripping down onto Tom's face as he withdrew a knife from a sheath strapped to his leg.

"I can see it in your eyes," the man said above him, blood dripping from his lips as he attempted to force the glinting blade down into Tom's face. "'Why won't this guy go down?'" Wells laughed, shaking his head ever so slowly, his face a bloody mess. "I can't feel a thing," he said. "Do you understand, boy? They made it so I don't feel any pain." The blade slowly descended. "It's a battle of the science projects," Wells grunted with exertion. "May the better freak win."

Finally Tom understood. But even though Wells couldn't feel pain, it didn't mean he couldn't be hurt— or killed. And now that Tom and Tyler had blended, becoming someone entirely new, Tom had no problem killing—not when it was necessary and not when he knew without a shadow of a doubt that the person deserved to die.

Bent backward over the desk, knife tip less than an inch from his eye, Tom lashed out, driving his heel into Wells's knee. The bones went with a muffled snap, and his attacker suddenly listed to one side, dropping to the floor, his leg no longer capable of supporting his weight.

As if sensing that this could be the final moment, Wells dropped his knife and dove for his discarded pistol. Sliding across the floor, he rolled onto his back and took aim, ready to fire.

But Tom was already there, landing in a crouch to straddle the man, driving the palm of his hand into Wells's already broken nose, sending a spear of cartilage up into the man's brain before he could pull the trigger. Wells dropped backward to the floor, eyes wide in death.

Tom took some solace in the fact that the man hadn't felt a thing.

His own body ached in places he hadn't even realized could hurt, but there was little time to worry about that. He left the room through the doorway where he'd first caught Kavanagh standing.

The former military facility was like a maze, and he navigated the gridwork of dimly lit concrete halls, prepared for anything. Tom slowed at the sound of something moving up ahead. Pressing his back against the cold concrete wall, he peered around the corner. He saw movement behind the metal cover over a ventilation shaft in the wall above. A kick to the cover caused it to pop loose from its screws and clatter noisily to the floor below. A pair of legs swung out from the shaft as a figure lowered itself to the hallway below it.

Tom stealthily moved forward, drawing back his hand to strike if necessary, but his presence was somehow detected—perhaps the shifting of his shadow on the wall ahead. The figure spun, gun in hand, aimed in his face.

"Fancy meeting you here," Victoria Lovett said, the hint of a smile instantly turning grim as she pulled the trigger.

CHAPTER 20

Victoria had fired off two rounds in rapid succession before Tom realized that she wasn't firing at him but at the two armed soldiers sneaking up on them from around the corner.

Tom found himself holding her wrist in such a way that the slightest amount of pressure could have snapped the bone neatly in two.

Victoria said nothing, looking into his eyes, waiting for him to set her free. He released her, going to the two dead soldiers and helping himself to their weaponry.

"Did you have to kill them?" he asked, fishing through their supply belts, searching for anything that could be useful.

"If I didn't, they would have killed you and probably me," she said coldly. "It's something that you learn in this game. No second thoughts: it's kill them before they can kill you."

The words were so severe coming out of the woman's mouth. It was hard to even imagine her as his mother anymore.

"Where are the others?" he asked, walking past her, continuing on his way down the hall. His number-one priority was to find Kavanagh, and she was slowing him down.

"Up above," she said. "On the base grounds. We encountered a welcoming committee and engaged in a little firefight. I'd guess they're probably wrapping things up now and will be down shortly."

Tom glared at her. "And what are you doing down here?" he asked.

"I slipped away when things got a little hairy," she said. "Nothing like an RPG blast to get people scrambling. I grabbed a gun from an unfortunate casualty and used a ventilation duct in one of the garage bays to get down here. A little advice: always familiarize yourself with the ductwork of any building you visit."

They carefully passed through a doorway to a metal walkway and a set of steps leading down to a lower level.

Tom started down the stairs ahead of her. "You still haven't answered my question," he said. "What are you doing here?"

"You know the answer to that, Tom," she said.

They reached the bottom of the stairs, and he turned and looked at her. "No, I don't. Why are you here?"

"There isn't time for this," she replied, shaking her head, obviously exasperated with the young man. "I knew you might need help . . . that you might be in danger. I wanted to help you . . . to show you that . . . to show you that I'm sorry for what I did."

Tom couldn't help but laugh. It was an unpleasant sound, void of any humor whatsoever. "You're sorry?" he asked mockingly. "You damn well should be."

She pushed past him, moving toward a cross section of corridors. "This isn't the time or place," she said. "I think we need to—"

"How could you do it?" he asked, feeling raw emotion bubbling to the surface. "I was . . . I was just a sick kid. How could you be part of something like that? What kind of person are you?"

Victoria turned, weapon in hand. It was surreal, the sight of the woman who had once meant so much to him, standing there, covered in grease, holding a gun as casually as a cell phone.

"I was a bad person. Is that what you want to hear, Tom? Okay, I've said it. I was a bad person."

"Was?"

She came toward him, and he resisted the urge to back away.

"I know it probably sounds like complete bull, but you changed me, Tom," Victoria said. "Being your mother was the single greatest experience I ever had."

She reached out, touching his face. He found that he couldn't pull away, almost as if he wanted her to touch him.

But that was crazy. She disgusted him.

Doesn't she?

"It started out as acting—a cover—but it turned into something much bigger than that. Believe me, I didn't want it to, but it happened."

Childhood memories flooded his mind, tender moments with his mother. He pulled his face away from her hand, stepping back. "I can remember all this stuff—with you, but how do I know it was even real?"

Victoria frowned, and he thought he might see tears in her eyes. "It's a terrible thing, how they treated you, Tom Lovett," she said, emotion resonating in her voice. "A terrible thing that I willingly took part in. And I know that it won't make up for even a fraction of what I did to you . . . to God knows how many other people in my less-than-legal activities over the years, but here is where I'm going to start."

Tom stared at her, torn. There was still a part of him

that despised her for what she had done and doubted that it was possible to ever forgive her completely, but there was another part, not quite as strong, that was willing to allow her to try and win back that lost trust.

It wasn't going to be easy for either of them.

"Which one?" he asked, moving around her toward the fork in the corridor. "Which one leads to Kavanagh's office?"

She looked at him then, saying nothing. For the moment, given the situation, they would accept each other. And after that?

They would just have to wait and see.

"Here," she said, pointing to the one on the left. "The place is like a maze, but I think his office and the labs are down this way."

"Labs?" Tom asked, a slight chill running up and down his spine.

"Yes," she said leading the way again. "Where our Mr. Kavanagh developed his . . . assets."

Tom followed, a growing sense of foreboding coursing through his veins.

The corridor came to an end at a set of double doors.

Tom cautiously approached them, craning his neck to look through the twin windows at the semidarkened room beyond.

The pneumatic doors parted with a hiss and he leapt back, gun at the ready, but it was only a sensor installed in the floor, reacting to his presence.

He looked at Victoria. She had stopped, a frown on her face.

"What's wrong?" he asked, a chill wafting out from the room ahead of them.

"I'm not sure you want to go in there," she said.

"Why?" Tom asked, turning back to the room, an intense anticipation building inside him, as if something of great importance was about to be revealed.

"Let's just say this is where a lot of your problems began."

And without hesitation, Tom entered, first noticing the strong smell of antiseptic. It reminded him of a hospital.

Violent flashes of memory froze him in place, images that he couldn't quite grasp entering his mind. Inexplicably, his mouth was filled with the taste of rubber as he painfully began to remember.

The room was designed in a circular fashion, as what could only have been a control center—computers, monitors, and machines right out of a science-fiction movie, all surrounding eight beds.

Tom bypassed the technology, moving beyond it to go directly to the beds. They seemed to call to him as he moved closer to investigate. Leather straps dangled from the sides of the empty beds, and suddenly he could feel them—a phantom memory—as the straps were pulled tight around his own wrists and ankles.

Tom's heartbeat quickened as he experienced the panic all over again—the taste of rubber in his mouth. He felt the prick of a needle in his arm as he struggled against the restraints.

This will help you sleep, he heard an echoing voice from the past say. But he didn't want to sleep; he wanted to know what they were going to do to him. His entire body had gone numb and they were putting things . . . putting wires inside his head.

In a trancelike state Tom touched his head, feeling beneath his sandy blond hair, feeling the slight bumps of scar tissue from the procedure on his scalp.

He remembered the faces of the medical staff standing over him, preparing him for . . .

Preparing me for what?

He didn't want to go to sleep—he'd learned to hate sleep, to fear it because of his illness—and fought futilely against the drugs that they had injected him with. And as he lost the battle against staying conscious, his panicked gaze fell on one face in particular—one face standing out in the crowd of men and women dressed in crisp white lab coats.

We're going to help you, the man had said, a friendly smile on his face. *We're going to make you . . .* special.

He hadn't known this man before, but he knew him now, having seen his face only moments ago.

Kavanagh.

A hand dropped down onto his shoulder, and he turned with a gasp to face Victoria.

"Are you all right?" she asked, giving his arm a gentle squeeze. Tom winced, still hurting from Wells's bullet earlier, but he didn't pull away, finding comfort in her touch.

He turned his head slightly to look at the empty beds. "What is this place?" he asked. "I can remember pieces, but I don't—"

"This is where they performed the procedure," she started to explain, all the while holding on to his arm, as if attempting to provide him with some of her strength. "Where the other identities were created."

Tom reached out to touch one of the pillows, the impression left by a head still evident. "I . . . I remember being here," he said with a mixture of realization and horror.

Victoria stood beside him. "I'm no scientist, but I believe they placed the subjects in a comalike state and then used a process to download information directly into their brains."

"How . . . how long were they . . . *was I* . . . ?" he asked, unable to take his eyes from the now-empty beds.

"I really don't know," Victoria answered. "Weeks . . . could have been months. The personality that would be the sleeper was implanted first, along with all the information and skills that would be required for him or her to perform special functions once activated. The other persona was given false memories, complex histories of lives never actually led."

He saw that she was staring as intently at the eight beds as he had. She seemed suddenly troubled, looking at to the floor.

"What's wrong?" he asked.

She reached down to the floor, picking up something and holding it up for him to see. It was one of the rubber mouth guards used to prevent the sleepers from biting their tongues while going through the implantation process. "It's . . . wet," she said.

Tom laid his hand on the bed.

"It's still warm," Tom said, his senses immediately becoming alert as he looked around the room. He imagined that the others would be warm as well.

"Where are they?" She asked the question before he could. "Where have the sleepers gone?"

And that was when they heard it. From somewhere

in a darkened corner something made a noise to let them know that they weren't alone.

Victoria raised her gun.

The first of the sleepers emerged from its hiding place, a child no more than ten years old dressed in powder blue hospital scrubs. It slowly stalked toward them, nothing even vaguely human registering in its eyes.

It's like looking into the eyes of a wild animal, Tom thought.

The others emerged, as if following the first's lead. There were seven in total, all dressed in a similar fashion, seeming to be around the same age. Probably the age he had been when awakened from the medically induced coma and placed in his handler's care.

The children with murder in their eyes approached them, and he turned to tell his mother to go—to leave and continue the search for Kavanagh while he stayed here and tried to find a way to save these kids from themselves. But he was startled to see that she was already on the way to the doors.

Tom was about to call out to her, unsure of how to react to the fact that she was leaving his side unprompted. The pneumatic doors parted, and Victoria Lovett left the chamber without turning around.

Did she betray me again? Tom wondered. *Abandon me to my fate?*

But that was a worry for another time, he told himself, turning his full attention back to the advancing sleepers.

Just as the first attacked.

Victoria moved away from the lab, heading off in search of Brandon Kavanagh.

She hated to leave Tom, she really did, but ultimately what she had to take care of was more important than sticking by his side for a battle she knew he could easily handle.

As she walked the cold concrete corridor, her mind wandered, and she recalled the first time she had met him. She had just completed a job acquiring the latest in microprocessor technology from a leading Japanese technology firm and selling it to their biggest rival. She'd made quite the killing and was thinking of slowing down, for at least as long as her bank balance would allow, when one of her brokers—the individuals who often found her jobs—arranged a meeting with the head of Janus.

And the rest was history.

The corridor suddenly became dark, and she noticed that the lights on the walls had been smashed. Alarm bells sounded in her head, but still she went on, driven by an overpowering sense of responsibility.

She'd had more than one meeting with the mysterious man, knowing at the time that he was part of a government agency specializing in the development and the international policing of high-risk technology. Victoria had found what he had to say fascinating and had been slowly drawn into his web.

The door to the office ahead was slightly ajar, a warm yellow light spilling out into the darkened hallway. She brought up her gun and, making sure that the safety was off, pushed open the door with her other hand, entering the room. It seemed to be empty, though his computer was still on and appeared to be performing some function.

Her curiosity took her around his desk to see what the computer was doing. She didn't even hear him come up from behind.

He was sneaky like that.

"Well, look who it is," she heard him say, and she quickly turned to face him. "I would have been here to greet you, but I was down the hall in the observation room, checking out what's going on in the lab. Seven against one; it just doesn't seem all that fair."

Victoria slid her gun into the waist of her pants and stepped toward him. "Didn't think I'd see you again after the last assignment you sent me on," she said, smiling seductively.

"Didn't go quite as planned, did it?" Kavanagh asked.

She shook her head. "Let's just say I needed to be at the top of my game to get here today."

"More so than usual?" he questioned, moving around her to get to the computer. "You *are* full of surprises, Victoria Lovett."

She shrugged, acknowledging his observation. "We'd better get going," she said, glancing at the watch on her wrist. "Pandora agents will be swarming in here in a matter of minutes. And I don't think *we* want to be here when they do."

Tom didn't want to hurt them, but the same couldn't be said of his attackers' attitudes toward him.

They were like wild dogs, the strongest of the pack attacking first while the others stayed back, watching with eager eyes.

The leader pounced, and Tom met the attack, placing his hands beneath the boy's arms and throwing him to one side. The boy landed catlike, bare feet slapping on the linoleum floor, crouched and ready to attack again.

Not giving him the chance, Tom went at him, putting the pack leader on the defensive. The first blow struck the boy in the face, knocking him to the floor. He quickly recovered, shaking off the effects of the blow and springing up with what could only be considered a growl on his lips.

The sleepers had no real technique, implying that they had not completed their training—that the download of information into their brains had been interrupted, making them less dangerous than they would have been otherwise. A good sign, meaning that Tom hopefully wouldn't have to fight them too long before he could subdue them enough to break them out of this place.

The leader lunged, a bestial ferocity burning in his eyes. No personality had yet been imprinted on the brains of these sleepers; raw, primal instinct was driving their actions along with what was likely Kavanagh's final command, downloaded into their brains, driving them into a killing frenzy as they were awakened.

Eliminate the intruder.

But he wasn't about to give them the chance.

The leader needed to be taken down first; quickly, efficiently, as an example to break the others' morale and to lower their confidence. Tom let him come in close, allowing him to land a few strikes—even draw blood.

The sight of blood seemed to excite the leader, making his actions more erratic—more unfocused. Tom saw that as his opportunity, bouncing back away from the boy and snapping out with his leg, his foot connecting with the leader's chest and sending him flying backward into the lab. Bouncing off a wall of storage lockers, the leader attempted to rise and then slumped to the floor, unmoving.

Tom turned to the others. They were looking back at him with cautious eyes, sizing him up.

Tom decided to help them out, running at them, attacking with a bloodcurdling scream. They were unprepared, almost on the verge of panic.

They attacked savagely, but he had them right where he wanted them, using their confusion to his advantage. They fought hard, kicking and throwing wild punches that could have killed Tom if they'd connected, but he wasn't about to let them succeed. He would not allow them to perform the function for which they had been created.

He would not allow them to become killers.

One by one he brought them down.

His body covered in blood and sweat, Tom found himself standing among the unconscious, only a single boy and girl of the sleeper pack remaining. The pair tensed, eyeing him, waiting for him to attack, but he held back.

"It doesn't have to be like this," he said in his calmest voice. "I don't want to fight anymore." He opened his scuffed and bloodied fists, extending his hands. "I want to help; do you understand?"

There was something in their expressions, some sign that deep down they were attempting to overpower the animalistic rage that had overtaken them on being roused from their artificial sleep.

"Please," he said, and started toward them.

The boy and girl watched him nervously. They were holding each other, their eyes roaming about the laboratory, their bodies trembling with fear.

"That's it," he said calmly, reaching out a reassuring hand. "I want to—"

The doors to the lab crashed violently open. Pandora soldiers swarmed into the room like locusts, weapons drawn.

"No!" Tom screamed, jumping in front of the young boy and girl, shielding them from harm.

The soldiers aimed their guns, squinting down the barrels of black metal weaponry as Christian Tremain strode into the room, Agent Abernathy loyally at his side.

"Stand down!" Tremain ordered, and the soldiers grudgingly obeyed.

The director looked around, a snarl forming on his face. "What the hell is this place?" he asked.

Tom wrapped his arms around the shivering pair. There was a moment's hesitation—their muscles stiffened, ready to attack—but as if sensing he meant them no harm, they allowed him to pull their trembling bodies against his.

"This is where I was born," he said, the enormity of the words hitting him with the force of a tidal wave. And he held the shivering children tighter, making a promise to himself that he would never allow something like this to happen again.

"That's that," Kavanagh said, and Victoria watched as he removed a disk from the computer tray, placing it carefully into a plastic case and then into his briefcase. "Let's go." He motioned her toward the door.

They walked side by side down a hallway toward a section of corridor that appeared to end abruptly with a concrete wall. She was about to say something wise, a crack about his sense of direction, when the wall slid aside at his approach.

He glanced briefly over his shoulder, a sly grin on his face.

"Coming?" he asked her, stepping through the entrance.

There was a metal staircase on the other side, leading down into what looked like some kind of private subway station. There was a sleek, bullet-shaped car on the track, waiting to take them both to freedom.

"Fancy," she said, eyeing the vehicle.

"Isn't it, though?" he commented. "It connects all the other installations in my network," he explained. "It's a maglev system: powerful magnets lift the carriage off the rails and propel it at about three hundred miles an hour."

His eyes twinkled at her as he spoke. "I've always hoped I'd get to use it."

He approached the craft, sliding an entrance hatch open to reveal a cockpit of sorts and four seats behind it. He tossed his briefcase inside.

"I hate to break it to you, but you're not," she said, pulling her gun and leveling the weapon at him. "Step back from the train," she instructed.

Kavanagh chuckled. "You can't be serious," he said.

And suddenly at that moment Victoria hated him more than she'd ever hated anyone. She hated him for all the obvious reasons, of course—the cruelty to which he had subjected the boy she perceived as her son being the most prominent—but she hated him most right then because he still believed, after everything she had been through, that she had remained loyal to him.

That I'm still one of the bad guys.

"You're working for *them* now?" he asked in disbelief. "How much are they paying? I'll double it."

Victoria shook her head. "Never thought I'd say the words, but it's not about the money anymore."

"Dear God, have you grown a conscience?" Kavanagh asked, feigning shock. "I know a few doctors who could remove that for you. . . ."

"Shut up, Brandon," she said, jabbing the gun toward him. "All the misery you're responsible for— what you've done to those poor kids—it's done. *I'm* done."

"'Those poor kids,'" he repeated, his eyes never leaving hers. "Or is it one kid in particular, Vicky?"

She said nothing, but he could read her—read her body language.

He chuckled and shook his head. "I've created a monster."

"Enough," she snapped. "Raise your hands and—"

Somewhere within the installation something exploded. It was a powerful, roaring sound in the distance, but it shook the very platform beneath her feet, causing her to momentarily lose her balance.

And then Kavanagh was upon her.

Tom was drawn to the sound of their voices.

He'd checked out Kavanagh's office and, finding it empty, had been ready to start his search for the founder of the Janus Project, to tear the place to the ground to find him—as well as Victoria Lovett.

Victoria. Tom clenched his jaw, struggling to make

sense of all the jumbled ideas and feelings her name alone brought up in him.

He thought about what Madison had told him soon after he regained consciousness aboard the transport plane. He'd awoken to find Madison right there beside him, holding his hand, and he'd squeezed back so tightly he was worried he'd hurt her. But Madison didn't let go, just smiled down at him, her eyes so warm and gentle. "I knew you'd come back to me, Tom," she'd said, and in that moment he understood that what they'd been through together had changed her as much as it had changed him—and had created an unbreakable connection between them.

Then Madison had asked Tom about Victoria, if it was possible for him to forgive her. He had been sure of his answer, positive that he would never allow himself to. Victoria Lovett was nothing but a lie.

But Madison had said maybe that wasn't totally true. She told him that after his capture at the Crypt, it had been Victoria who had sat with him, holding his hand, just as Madison was doing then.

Victoria had been acting just like a real mother.

Tom gave his head a shake, trying to clear out the confusion and focus. There would be time to deal with all of this later, when Kavanagh's plans were stopped and he was finally in Pandora custody or dead.

Standing in the doorway, preparing to head back in the direction he had come, he thought he heard the sound of voices coming from the end of a corridor that at first glance seemed to be a dead end. He moved carefully toward the darkened section of hallway and found the entrance into the chamber beyond.

Stepping through onto the metal staircase, Tom took in the sight of the underground transport station as well as Victoria holding Kavanagh at gunpoint.

Tom immediately felt a sense of relief, thoughts of the woman's further betrayal of him dissolving like smoke. He had started down the stairs to aid her when he felt the explosion. The metal staircase shook violently underneath him, nearly pitching him over the side, and as he regained his balance, he saw the situation below go to critical.

Kavanagh had made his move. He grabbed Victoria's arm, pulling it back behind her body and wresting the gun from her hand.

"No!" Tom screamed at the top of his lungs, throwing himself down the staircase with a stumbling grace.

"Not another step closer," the man warned, jamming the weapon against Victoria's neck.

Tom stopped, but his instincts did not. Almost immediately he was processing every scenario of how to remove Victoria from danger. Most of what he could attempt was too risky. He had to wait.

"Tyler's gone, isn't he?" Kavanagh said.

Tom shook his head. "He isn't gone; he's inside me—everything that he knew, everything that he was, whether good or bad, is part of me now."

Kavanagh smiled at him, revealing little warmth or humor. "That's all pretty amazing," he said. "We'd never planned for anything like you, but it doesn't change what you actually are—what you were created to be."

Victoria struggled momentarily. "Tom, don't listen to him. He—"

"Shut your mouth," Kavanagh hissed, yanking her arm farther back.

The woman yelped in pain.

"You're a weapon; you were created to kill. That's all you were ever meant to be." Kavanagh paused; letting his words sink in. "Bet you could rattle off a least a hundred ways to kill me in under three seconds."

"Two," Tom said, his anger sparking. "I could think of a hundred ways to kill you in two seconds."

The head of the Janus Project laughed. "A wicked sense of humor," he said. "I like that. I made sure that they gave one to Tyler when they were filling in all his blanks. But it doesn't change what you'll always be."

The lights in the tunnel flickered, and from somewhere in the distance they heard something that sounded like thunder—but they knew that it wasn't. It was gunfire, and it was drawing closer.

Tom stepped forward, and Kavanagh started to pull Victoria backward toward the bullet car.

"So what's your favorite, Tyler—or do you prefer Tom? If you could kill me now, which one of the hundred ways would be your preference?"

"It doesn't have to be like this," Tom said, an almost-palpable tension growing in the air.

"I bet you'd prefer to use your hands," Kavanagh said. "Can't get any more up close and personal than that."

"I won't kill you unless I have to," Tom told him without hesitation. "Let the woman go, surrender your weapon, and you get to keep your life."

Kavanagh shook his head in wonder. "Listen to you," he said. "So merciful. Maybe you actually have turned into something more than a killer"

He continued to back toward the train. "I think I'm going to try a little experiment here," he said. "Let's see if you actually are more than I say."

Tom tensed. He was ready to move, to throw himself at Kavanagh, pushing all three of them into the vehicle. He hoped he would have the opportunity to disarm the man and . . .

"Let's see," Kavanagh said, and the sound of three muffled shots filled the air.

Tom watched in horror as blossoms of crimson erupted on Victoria's chest. Then he screamed, rushing forward as Kavanagh roughly shoved her limp body toward him. He caught her in his arms, lowering her gently to the ground. The amount of blood seeping from her wounds was overpowering, and he placed his hands over the leaking holes in a futile attempt to stop the bleeding.

"Oh my God," he said over and over again. He knew a hundred ways to take someone's life in seconds, but he didn't have the slightest clue how to save one.

The sound of rapid gunfire was closer now; it wouldn't be long until the Pandora troops arrived. But they were too late.

"What did you do?" he asked, cradling the woman in his arms. She was convulsing now, blood leaking from her mouth. He was helpless—totally helpless as he watched her life slip away. "What did you do?"

He turned his rage-filled eyes from the dying woman to Brandon Kavanagh, who stood in the doorway of the futuristic train.

"I'm going to kill you," Tom spat, his body trembling with fury and complete and utter sorrow.

"I thought you would have done that by now," the

man said, frowning sadly as he nodded slowly. "Maybe there is something more to you."

And Kavanagh closed the doors, disappearing from view as he readied his escape.

Pandora soldiers descended the metal staircase, filling the chamber as the escape vehicle began to hum, rising ever so slightly to hover above the tracks momentarily before it pulled away from the station, the craft rocketing down the darkened tunnel, barely making a sound as it left the installation with their quarry.

Kavanagh was gone, but Tom didn't care.

Tom held the woman he'd once known as his mother in his arms and felt her life slowly slipping away. In the background he heard the soldiers yelling for a medic, but he knew that she had passed beyond that point. It was only a matter of time now before she was gone.

Her eyes were closed but suddenly came open, focusing on him.

"So . . . sorry," she said, a fresh stream of red bubbling up from the corner of her mouth. "I . . . I never meant to love you," she said, reaching a blood-covered hand up to touch his face. "Just happened."

Tom took her hand in his and, bringing it to his mouth, gently kissed it, his inner conflict dissolving away. Now wasn't the time for anger.

"It's all right," he told her, feeling her breathing grow shallow. "I forgive you."

Her eyes began to close again.

"I love you, Mom," he said, pulling her close and whispering in her ear, wanting with all his heart for those to be the last words she heard as she left him.

Falling into the embrace of death.

Tom imagined it was very much like going to sleep.

In a room at the Hotel Assa, in Nazran, Igushetia—
Chechnya—Brandon Kavanagh motioned for the man
to roll up the sleeve of his shirt.

He appeared nervous and rightfully so, looking to
his three superiors for some sort of reprieve. But it
didn't come, his commanders silently urging him to do
as he was asked.

The Chechen soldiers had lost their battle for inde-
pendence against the Russians, but they still continued
to fight and to die, these freedom fighters' dreams filled
with the day they would at last have the ability to strike
back at their usurpers with a fury that would drive the
enemy from their beloved land.

Which was why Kavanagh was there.

He was all about the fulfillment of dreams.

From a small briefcase he removed the syringe—a small sample of the wish fulfillment he had to offer.

In the soldier's native tongue Kavanagh told the man it wouldn't hurt a bit and then laughed, bringing the tip of the needle to the man's arm and injecting the gold-colored fluid into his veins.

The drug was something he had been in the process of developing before Janus—something that he had always believed could be a healthy fallback if things should go wrong with his primary focus. It was a derivative of the same treatment that had made Noah Wells immune to pain. But this drug would also enhance strength, endurance, speed, and aggression. A consistent regimen of injections could create an army of virtual super-soldiers, ready to take on and defeat just about any opposing force.

Kavanagh didn't bother to explain that constant use of the drug would cause madness and excruciating withdrawal, eventually leading to death; minor bumps in the road on the journey to granting wishes as far as he was concerned.

The soldier's eyes rolled back in his head as the narcotic flowed through his bloodstream, his flesh almost immediately breaking out in beads of perspiration. Kavanagh had shown them video recordings of the drug in use, but before committing to the deal, the Chechens had demanded to see an example of the drug's effects on one of their own. And like any good businessman, he had obliged them.

Kavanagh despised what his life had become: hiding himself and his business away, selling the high-tech weaponry secretly acquired during his years with Pandora in the most godforsaken, war-torn places in the world. He couldn't afford to be on the radar again; he needed to keep his head low, amassing the funds that he would need to begin his practices anew.

Until then he would deal with any two-bit army or renegade warlord that had the funds to buy his wares.

"Is it working?" the casually dressed older man, who he'd learned was actually a general, asked in between puffs of his foul-smelling cigar.

"It takes a minute or two," Kavanagh said, closing up the briefcase and handing it off to his bodyguard and driver, looking menacing as he stood coolly beside his chair.

The soldier appeared to be asleep, his head lolling loosely on his shoulders as the drug wormed its way through his system. He wouldn't receive the full benefit of the narcotics with only one injection, but there would be enough of a change to prove that the drug was worth its expense.

The soldier's eyes suddenly snapped open, and an enormous grin spread across his features.

"How do you feel?" the general asked his soldier, hovering over the man as if searching for some hint of physical change.

The soldier reached up to snatch the lit cigar from his commanding officer's mouth. He smiled maniacally, puffing on the cigar's wet end before placing the hot tip against the palm of his hand, the flesh producing an oily black smoke as it started to burn.

"How do I feel?" the soldier asked. "Like I could take on the world."

And that was all the general needed to hear.

The transaction took no longer than five minutes, the cost for the first batch of the enhancement drug being electronically transmitted to a secret account set up in a Zurich bank.

The Chechens were the first to leave the hotel room, eager to return to the war-torn countryside to show the Russian Special Forces that the war was far from over.

Kavanagh waited just over ten minutes before leaving himself, allowing his bodyguard to step from the room first out into the shadowy hall. He pulled the door closed behind him and turned to see a member of the hotel's cleaning staff, a pretty red-haired young woman, coming down the hallway pushing a cart of towels and fresh linens toward him.

He smiled politely, and she did the same, wishing him a good morning as they passed.

It is indeed a good morning, he thought, pleased that the transaction had gone without incident, moving him that much closer to even better days ahead.

It's truly amazing how quickly life changes, Madison Fitzgerald thought, wheeling the fresh linens cart down the hallway of the Chechen hotel.

"Good morning," she said to the target, remembering to use the accent taught to her by her language coach back at the Pandora Group.

A little over two years ago she'd been in Chicago, fighting with her parents over the fact that they were sending her to Massachusetts to live with her aunt and uncle.

And look at her now.

"Target has been sighted and confirmed," she said softly, speaking into a tiny microphone disguised as the top button on her maid's uniform. "Repeat, target has been sighted and confirmed."

After her involvement with the Janus affair and her parents' incapacitation as a result, she had been temporarily placed in the home of Pandora agent Catherine

Mayer, finishing up her senior year of high school before enrolling in a special Pandora training program.

Director Tremain had done his best to persuade her otherwise, even bribing her with the offer of a full scholarship to Harvard or Yale, but she would hear nothing of it. She had gotten a glimpse of a world very few people even dreamed of, and it had changed her.

How could it not? She had seen parts of herself she never knew existed and wanted to explore them. And besides, Pandora was where Tom was.

She stopped the cart mid-hall, removing the pistol hidden beneath the stack of towels and placing it in the front pocket of the apron she was wearing. Then she headed for the stairs.

"Subject has been sighted," said a voice in her ear that made her heart beat faster. "Proceeding with appre-hension protocol," Tom Lovett said over the airwaves.

And she found herself quickening her descent down the many flights of hotel stairs, a knot of apprehension forming in the pit of her stomach.

Madison knew how much Tom hated Brandon Kavanagh and had to wonder if it would be possible for him to separate his feelings to capture this man and bring him to justice. Or would the killer instinct that had become part of his makeup assert itself?

· · ·

The air embraced him as soon as he stepped from the hotel lobby into the cold.

Kavanagh pulled the collar of his heavy woolen overcoat up around his neck and looked toward the steel gray sky. *Looks like snow,* he thought, hoping to be gone before it began.

He felt their eyes on him and turned to see three children standing in the street nearby, watching. They had been playing with a soccer ball in the debris-strewn Nazran street, but now they just watched him.

His driver waited patiently, blowing into his bare hands for warmth against the damp Chechen cold. Kavanagh pulled his own leather gloves from his coat pockets and slipped them over his hands as he started toward the man. Together they turned down the alley that ran between the Hotel Assa and the burnt-out remains of what looked at one time to have been a grocery store. Normally at this time of day there would have been a police presence or at least some Russian soldiers on patrol, but he had made sure that the proper authority had been paid off, guaranteeing him the time required to do his business unhindered.

His driver opened the back passenger door of the black sedan, and he slipped into vehicle, adjusting his coat beneath him on the cold leather seat.

Kavanagh sat, waiting for the driver to appear in his

seat up front, but the man didn't enter the car. Annoyed, he turned, trying to look outside the frosty windows, but all he could see was the dark, dirty brick of the alley. He pushed open the door and got out, heading around the car. Suddenly his annoyance turned to shock as he nearly tripped on the body of his driver, lying on the ground in front of the driver's side door.

"What the hell is . . . ?"

And then he noticed them, just up ahead in the alley, the three children, two boys and a girl, no older than twelve or thirteen, staring at him just as they had done from the street.

And as they started down the alley and he studied their strange, dispassionate faces, Brandon Kavanagh came to the horrific realization that he knew them.

An image flashed before his mind's eye of the children restrained in hospital beds, crying pitifully as they were drugged unconscious.

Sleepers.

His hand went to his coat pocket for the gun that he always carried. He had brought the weapon out, ready to fire, when there was a glint of something shiny and a sudden sharp burning pain in his hand. Kavanagh dropped the pistol to the ground and stared in horror at the sight of a Japanese throwing star, one of its razor-sharp points embedded in the back of his glove as well as the soft flesh beneath.

He reached out, pulling the star from his hand, and turned to run—then came to an abrupt stop as he saw that the end of the alley was blocked by four more children.

And a young man with murder in his eyes.

Tom Lovett stood at the entrance to the alleyway, at last face-to-face with the man who had taken so much from him.

He'd thought about this moment every day since Kavanagh had escaped two years ago.

He watched as Kavanagh's eyes darted frantically around him, increasingly panicked as he realized he was trapped.

The newest children of Janus had emerged from their mechanical wombs devoid of humanity, equipped only with the rudimentary knowledge of how to kill. They, too, had been taken under Pandora's wing, and Pandora—with Tom's help—had done what they could to bring back the children's true personalities. But as with himself, the killer instinct had been activated in these kids; there was nothing anybody could do to take that away. So with Tremain's guidance these children had become Tom's team, and today they were about to take down the most elusive of targets.

Kavanagh lunged for his discarded gun, and the children beside Tom began to move.

"No," he ordered them, already striding toward the man.

This was something he had to do on his own.

Kavanagh snatched up the gun from the ground and spun around, but Tom was practically upon him. He saw the man's finger twitch on the trigger of the Beretta nine millimeter, changing his path to avoid the bullet even before it had left the barrel of the gun.

Dodging death, he remembered everything, brain crackling, his fury fueled by the memory of the events that had brought him to this point.

You're a weapon, the man before him had said the last time they had met. *Created to kill.*

Tom reached Kavanagh before another shot could be fired, ripping the gun from his grasp.

That's all you were ever meant to be.

He turned Kavanagh's weapon on him, sighting down the barrel of the gun at a place directly between his eyes. Tom's finger stroked the metal of the trigger, seduced by the moment he had been waiting for.

A moment he was no longer certain he had the strength to make happen.

Meant to be.

"Do it," Kavanagh hissed, leaning forward to press his forehead to the barrel of the gun. "Do what you were created to do."

From out of the corner of his eye Tom saw a flurry of movement as someone slowly approached. He imagined that Madison was curious if he had the strength as well.

"Kill . . ."

He had been this man's puppet, a weapon of flesh and blood trained in the art of death, but not anymore.

". . . me!" Kavanagh commanded him.

Tom Lovett wasn't an instrument of murder anymore. He was nobody's puppet—nobody's weapon.

The expression on Kavanagh's face as Tom removed the gun barrel from his head was priceless. He stepped back, putting the Beretta into his jacket pocket.

"What are you doing?" Kavanagh asked.

"This is Sleeper One, Pandora," Tom said, pressing his hand to a tiny earpiece. "Suspect has been apprehended; prepare for immediate retrieval."

"That's an affirmative, Sleeper One." He heard the sound of Christian Tremain's voice in his ear. "Good job."

Madison Fitzgerald smiled warmly as Tom approached. He stood beside her, and she reached down to give his hand a secret squeeze of support, their fingers inter-twining together behind his back.

Tom watched the Janus children quickly restrain Kavanagh, dragging him screaming toward the black van that suddenly came screeching around the corner.

As the kids forced him inside the back of the van, Kavanagh struggled in their grasp, turning around to look at Tom.

You're a weapon, created to kill. That's all you were ever meant to be, the final look in Brandon Kavanagh's eyes said as he disappeared inside the belly of the van.

But Tom knew otherwise.

He was so much more than that.

Acknowledgments

Ginormous piles of thanks and love to LeeAnne for the help she provided on this book and to Mulder for not throwing me out of his house.

Thanks are also due to Chris Golden for being a great friend and listener, Liesa Abrams for being such a great editor and being too damn cute for words, Margaret "Madge" Wright for her *interesting* insight, and Eloise Flood for being the cat's pajamas.

Great gobs of gratitude also go to Mom and Dad, Mom and Dad Fogg, David Kraus, Ken Curtis, Kim and Abby, David Carroll, Jon and Flo, Bob and Pat, Jean Eddy, Pete Donaldson, Jay Sanders, Eric Powell, Don Kramer, Greg Skopis, and Tim Cole and the dudes at Cole's Comics.

Farewell and adieu.